Magic Mirror

The Traveler's Tale

Luther Tsai
Nury Vittachi

REYCRAFT
BOOKS

Reycraft Books
55 Fifth Avenue
New York, NY 10003

Reycraftbooks.com

Reycraft Books is a trade imprint and trademark of Newmark Learning, LLC.

Library of Congress Cataloging-in-Publication data is available.

ISBN: 978-1-4788-6811-8

Printed in Guangzhou, China
4401/0919/CA21901492
10 9 8 7 6 5 4 3 2 1

First Edition Paperback published by Reycraft Books 2019

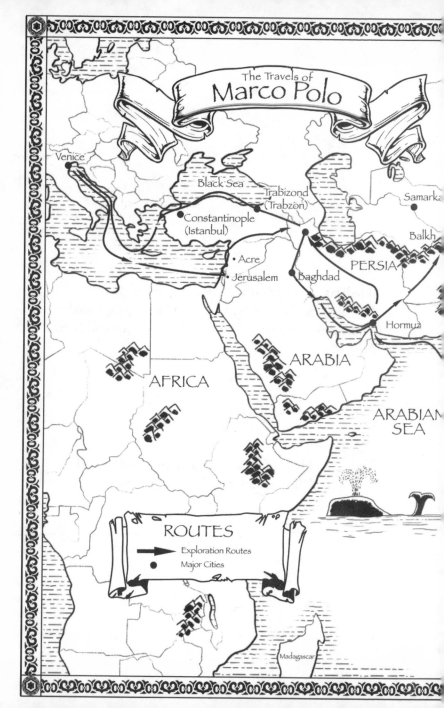

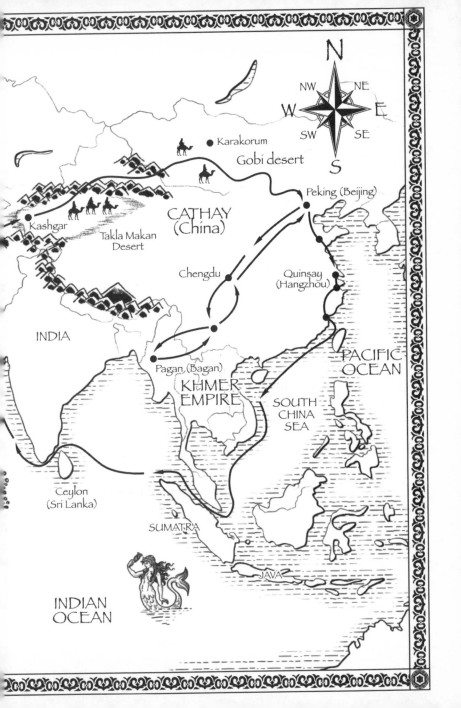

What Is Real?

I believe it was God's will that we should come back
so that people might know the wonderful things
that are in the world.

—Marco Polo

Look inside the Magic Mirror ...

Non ho scritto la metà di quello che ho visto.
(I have not told half of what I saw.)
—Marco Polo's last words when asked about his travels

CONTENTS

Page

Odd Encounters

Huh? Uh-oh. Now this was weird. Someone was following him. Like in a movie.

A short, chubby person trailed around 150 feet behind him, walking at the same pace, and keeping in the same position, even when he crossed the road.

Bizarre. It was the sort of thing that happened in spy dramas, not to kids in real life, Marko Lee thought. He MUST be imagining it, surely? The boy, continuing to stroll down the street, decided he had to do an experiment to find out one way or another.

He stopped abruptly, turned to face the road, and waited for a gap in the traffic. The guy apparently tailing him also stopped.

Then Marko carefully crossed the road and started walking back the way he had come. So did his tail. Now that was clear confirmation. It wasn't his imagination. He really was being followed.

After about half a minute, Marko stopped and dropped to the ground, pretending to tie his shoelaces. It gave him a chance to look behind him.

The guy following him stopped and pretended to tie his shoelaces too … except he was wearing slip-ons!

Marko got a good look at him, albeit upside down. His first impression had been of a large child, shorter but broader than he was, but now he could see that it was a very short man—chubby and pink, with an upturned nose.

But what should he do? Perhaps just speak to him. It was an option they never chose in the movies, but it seemed the logical thing to do.

"You following me?" Marko asked, standing up and turning to face him.

"What? No … uh … the man," the little man said, flustered.

"Why are you following me?" Marko continued.

"No particular reason," the pink man said, glancing behind him, and taking a step back.

"Would you mind not following me?"

"OK, no problem, not that I am."

Marko took one sudden step forward, the way you do when you want to scare a dog.

The man jumped. Then he turned and scampered rapidly away.

The boy stood and watched, baffled. He felt faintly insulted by the fact that he was being followed by such an amateur. Why was I assigned such a useless pursuer? Am I not worth someone better?

But he realized there was a bigger mystery here. Why was he being followed at all? Who was the man, and why had he been so scared? Was he, puny, bookish Marko Lee, beginning to look dangerous? He peered at his left bicep. I must be getting bigger and stronger, he said to himself. Maybe it's all that ice cream. Ice cream has milk in it, right? He resolved to tell his sister about it.

* * *

Aarrgghh! Miranda Lee scrunched up her hands into fists. But she had no one to thump but herself. Her problem was inside her head.

The trouble with secrets, she'd discovered, is that the pesky things won't stay secret. They should disappear quietly into some sort of locked compartment at the back of your head, silent and invisible, as if they'd never existed at all.

But no. Instead, they jump around, banging on your skull from the inside ... and then keep trying to leak out by finding their way to your mouth, sometimes even reaching the tip of your tongue.

Her friends had been talking about venues for a birthday party, comparing the sizes of their homes and apartments. In such conversations, Mira kept her mouth tightly shut. Everyone knew she lived in an old, musty, smelly, run-down house with eccentric parents, an aged grandfather, and a younger brother—not an acceptable venue for a cool party.

But *all* the adults in her house had vanished indefinitely. On the face of it, this was a rather worrying development, since she and her brother were mere children, after all; but when seen in the light of party locations, it was great news. Her home may have become the perfect place in which young people could play loud music and stay up half the night giggling.

"You could come to my place," her mouth said, before her brain could stop it.

There was a moment of silence. No one spoke, but the response was clear from their horrified eyes, which appeared to say: "Ew, no thanks, it's a horrible, smelly, musty old house filled with severely uncool people."

In her defense, she added, "Yes, but the thing is, just now, there are no ad—" and that was the point at which Mira's common sense reached her mouth and clamped it shut. She rapidly changed tack. "You're right. Let's have it at Sam's place like last time."

* * *

A minute later, Mira decided to head back into the classroom before break time was officially over. It was easier to keep her secrets during class time, when there was always an "official" topic on which to focus. In the formless chatter of the playground, things on one's mind could too easily slip out.

On the way up the stairs, she saw her little brother and decided to vent her frustrations on him instead. "You haven't told anyone, have you? It's really important that you put it right out of your mind, understand?"

"Put what right out of my mind?"

"You know. *The Thing.*"

"What thing?"

"About *you know what.*"

"What?"

He was so irritating. She looked right and left and dropped her voice to a whisper. "About Grandpa. About Mama and Daddy."

"What about your mother and father?" said a deeper voice behind her. "Something wrong?"

Mira spun around.

The mathematics teacher Mr. Aldred was standing behind her. He must have crept up behind her. He was very tall and very bearded and very scary. "Something wrong?" he repeated, in his low, growly voice. "With your parents?"

"Nothing, nothing," she said, smiling at the teacher. "They're at home, er, as usual, every day, all day, waiting for us, each and every night. And Grandpa. I mean, it's not like they're missing or anything, ha ha ha." She glared at her brother one more time before marching off.

If she was angry with herself before, now she was incensed. "Stupid, stupid, stupid," she said to herself as she marched down the corridor. Had she said something that would lead Mr. Aldred to guess that they were guardianless, with Mama, Daddy, and Grandfather all having vanished?

But then she consoled herself by arguing that if she had, it would all be her brother's fault for being so unreliable that she had to check on him constantly.

The bell rang to signify the end of break. "Thank goodness," she said out loud.

She stomped into her classroom and slumped into her chair.

* * *

Marko stood at the window of his classroom, looking at the school gates. In the distance, he could see a few parents standing around chatting, and a postman cycling down the street.

He looked for the scared short man, but couldn't see him. What on earth had that been all about? Ever since Grandpa had disappeared, life had become increasingly bizarre. And Marko had the feeling that the strangeness was only just beginning.

Secrets Shared

By the end of the school day, Miranda Lee had made a big decision. Instead of struggling with her impossible-to-keep secret, she was just going to tell one person—someone she could really trust. That would let the pressure out of her head without causing trouble, she hoped.

And so, ten minutes after the final bell had rung, she sat in a classroom with her favorite teacher, Ms. Modi, who taught art.

"You must promise not to tell anyone," the girl said.

Ms. Modi nodded. "You can certainly speak to me in confidence, Mira," she said. "But do remember that there are some things that teachers have to reveal to the authorities. For example, if someone's safety is at stake."

Mira thought for a moment. "I don't think there's a safety issue."

For the next ten minutes, she told Ms. Modi about the absence of the adults in her household. Her parents had gone off four or five weeks ago on a business trip, leaving them with their grandfather. Her mother and father often traveled together for work, so there was nothing unusual about this.

But the problem was that Grandfather had then gone off on a trip himself, less than a week later, and failed to return. So the two children had been living by themselves for a month now.

"We have a lady who comes in and does some cleaning and cooking three times a week, so the house is not like totally wrecked, and there's food in the fridge," Mira said. "But no grown-ups. We go to bed when we like, we eat ice cream for breakfast, and so on."

"When are your parents due back?"

The girl's face dropped. "Well, that's just it. Something strange happened last night." She paused, suddenly reluctant to continue.

The teacher leaned forward. "Go on. But first, tell me, where are they?"

"I don't know. They're in the Congo, or the Amazon rain forest, or Irian Jaya, or somewhere like that, with no Internet or mobile phone connections. They're always doing that sort of thing. Anyway, last night Mama managed to get an international line and phoned us."

"So you told her that Grandpa had left and you had no one to look after you? You told her to hurry back?"

Mira shook her head and looked genuinely puzzled. "That's the weird thing. I was going to. I had been praying for her to call so I could say just that. But as soon as I heard her voice, I felt really angry for some reason. So instead, I just said we were fine. I was really snotty. Then I handed the phone to my brother and he said the same thing. I don't know why we did that. After waiting so long to hear from them, it was weird. I just wanted to get them off the line."

Ms. Modi nodded slowly.

The girl went on: "It's almost as if I didn't want them to come back. But that would be really bad, wouldn't it, if I felt like that?"

The teacher put her hand gently on her student's shoulder. "Don't worry, Mira," she said. "It's a natural reaction. Children have a right to be looked after. When your guardians let you down, you go through various stages of emotion, starting with fear and disappointment, and moving to anger. That's probably where you're at."

They talked about it for several minutes, and what the teacher said seemed to make sense. She said the two of them were naturally feeling annoyed because they had been abandoned by the guardians who were supposed to be looking after them. It would be odd for them to have reacted any other way.

Ms. Modi added, "Now, if you had been a year younger, I would be legally required to tell the authorities that you and your brother were home alone. Instead, I'm not going to say anything, but I'll phone you every evening, to make sure you're OK. And if your grandfather or your parents are not home by the end of the week, we'll investigate properly, and start contacting people."

Mira smiled. "You don't have to do that. Well, you could phone or visit occasionally if you like. It's kind of quiet in the evenings. Also, I wanted someone to have a spare house key in case we lock ourselves out, and I'd like that person to be you."

"Fine. I'd be delighted. I'm glad you talked to me. I've been worried. You haven't been your usual self."

The conversation seemed to have reached its natural conclusion, but Mira didn't move.

"There's something else, isn't there?" the teacher asked.

The girl nodded. "Some weird things have been happening. I've had crazy dreams. Marko says he sees odd creatures in the garden. Like gnomes or something. And on the third night of being by ourselves, we were in Grandpa's study looking at his books and this strange thing he has, called a magic mirror ..." She bit her bottom lip.

"Go on."

"Well, this is going to sound mad, but I'll say it anyway. The mirror is really a sort of thin, metal light filter. We held it up to the moonlight, and the light projected images on the walls behind us. It was like being in a ship's cabin."

"That sounds wonderful. Can you bring it to school? I'd love to see it."

"Yes. They have them at some museums, so you've probably seen one without realizing it. But ... well, the thing is, in this case, the room really seemed to become a ship's cabin."

"Oh, the joy of having a child's imagination," said Ms. Modi. "I wish I could do that."

"No, it seemed really real," said Mira. "It wasn't just imagination. We were on a ship. We met people, talked to them, lived with them for days. We even found out what ship it was. It was the Treasure Ship, the one commanded by Zheng He, you know? The famous explorer? You probably think it sounds crazy."

Ms. Modi smiled. "Quite the opposite. I'd be surprised if it hadn't happened."

Mira stared. This had not been the response she expected.

The teacher continued, "This is exactly what happens if you eat the wrong things all the time. Ice cream for breakfast, come on! You were probably having the worst sugar overload in history. You're sitting in your grandfather's study with all his books about exploration, and you had a dream or even some sort of hallucination."

"If it was a dream, Marko had it too."

"He was in your dream? Or you both dreamed about the same thing? That's not unusual. Forget about it. And eat proper food. It'll stop the bad dreams. I'll bring some around if you want."

Mira shook her head. "No need, there's food in the fridge."

There was a knock at the door. It opened and a young man looked in.

The teacher nodded at him, but spoke to Mira. "They need this classroom for after-school pottery," she said. "We need to move. Are you going to be OK?"

Mira smiled and nodded.

It was nice to feel cared for by an adult again.

Curious Visitors

On Thursday evening, there was a loud *rat-a-tat-tat* on the door.

Miranda looked up from her meal. In an attempt to take Ms. Modi's advice, she had served her brother and herself a healthy, balanced meal, the sort grownups prepared. As well as microwaving some rice and chicken from the fridge, she had added vegetables and even some salad, although she doubted whether either of them would eat all of it.

Then she had placed the food on the table, and made her little brother turn off the TV. To her surprise, he obeyed, scampering to the table and sitting formally in his chair.

"We have to behave exactly as our parents taught us to," she said. "It's very important to keep up the appearance of normality." She had heard the phrase somewhere on a TV show, and it seemed to fit the situation.

To her surprise, he didn't complain, and he ate all the vegetables and the salad, too.

This inspired her to do the same, and she found that green beans and lettuce actually tasted pretty good. She guessed that her body needed these things, and had been feeling deprived. That's what parents should do, she thought, deliberately deprive children of vegetables and then offer them some once a week, when their bodies were craving them.

That was when the knocking started at the front door.

"Who's that?" she asked.

"I don't know," replied Marko, continuing to eat and read, as was his habit. He was lost in an illustrated book on his current favorite topic, extreme weather phenomena.

"Go get the door. I got dinner."

"But—" He was about to object, but then appeared to change his mind. "OK." Taking one more mouthful of salad, he hopped off the chair and went to the front of the house.

After half a minute, Mira, curious, hopped off her chair and ran after him. She saw that her brother had opened the door but left the chain fastened. Through the gap she saw a small, fat, nervous man.

"It's you," said Marko.

"Yes," said the man, stepping back and sniffing with his piggy little nose. "It is me. In person."

"What do you want?"

"I ... I ... I'm here to announce the arrival in your lives of Mr. Singe."

Mira pushed her brother out of the way and took over the conversation. To start with, she decided to shut the door, release the chain, and open it again. The man was so small and so nervous that it was impossible to think of him as dangerous.

"I am the head of the household at this moment," she announced in her most grown-up voice. "The other members are not available. Please come back next week, Mr. Singe."

The man blinked. "I am not Mr. Singe."

"But you said ..."

"Mr. Singe is behind me. He likes to be announced."

"You have to ring before you come. You can't just turn up at someone's house. It's not … good manners."

"Mr. Singe has something for you. A letter. It must be delivered by hand to the right person."

They peered behind him, but there was no one to be seen.

"Where is he?" Marko asked.

The chubby man looked up.

The oddest man they had ever seen dropped from the sky. He had been sitting in a tree in the front garden. As he approached them, they saw he had thin limbs and walked with bent knees so that the hands at the ends of his long arms reached right down to his shins. He had a big, round jaw and an almost completely flat nose. He looked like a human monkey.

"Mrs. Lee? Very pleased to meet you. And this must be Mr. Lee." Mr. Singe had a high, squeaky voice. "This is for you." He held out a large envelope.

Miranda felt outraged. "I'm not Mrs. Lee. I'm twelve. And that's my little brother. He's ten."

Mr. Singe looked annoyed. "You're not? Oh. Well, can you fetch them?"

"They're out," she said, before remembering that children were not supposed to admit things like that to strangers. "Look, I'll take it for them. Thanks."

The long-limbed man lifted the letter out of her reach. "But he was very specific. Very, very specific. It had to be delivered to Mr. Lee the younger or Mrs. Lee. Placed in their hands. A matter of the utmost urgency, he said. A matter of life and death, literally."

"They're out," said Marko. "You can either give it to us or go away." He started to shut the door. "Take it back to wherever it came from."

The small, pink man looked alarmed. "We can't go back. No, no, no. Give it to them, please, Mr. Singe, give it to them."

Mr. Singe also looked worried. "Do you think we should, Mr. Cochon?"

"I don't know," said the little man. "You decide. You're bigger."

"But you're older."

Marko started to shut the door again.

"OK, we'll give it to you, but you'll have to sign for it," said Mr. Singe.

Marko opened the door wide.

Mira stepped forward. "I'll do that," she said, "as current head of the household."

Mr. Singe gave her a pen and pointed to his forearm. "Sign here," he said.

She wrote her name on his thin, bony, hairy arm, and he handed her the envelope.

"Where's the rest of it?" she asked, noticing that it had apparently been ripped in two.

The apelike man scrunched up his hat in his hands apologetically. "The Greddish got that. I'm sorry. We saved most of it."

Then the two visitors turned and left.

"Is it from our grandfather? Where is he?" Marko shouted out behind them.

"Oh, we can't tell you that," said Mr. Singe, breaking into a run. "Open the letter."

"What's the Greddish?"

But the men pretended they were out of earshot, and very soon really were.

The Mission

What weird people," said Mira.

"The little one followed me to school this morning," her brother said.

"Mr. Cochon."

"Yes. Let's look inside ... it must be from Ye Ye."

And so it proved. The handwriting on the front of the letter was unmistakable.

Mira moved toward the study, but Marko objected. "Hey! You said we had to behave like we did if Mama and Daddy were here. They wouldn't let us leave the table halfway through dinner to open a letter."

A little grid of irritation appeared between Mira's eyebrows. *Grrr.* "But they're not here," she argued. She knew he was right though. After a moment's pause, she walked back with him to the dining table, where they quickly finished eating with the torn letter sitting in front of them.

As soon as they'd both taken their last mouthfuls, Mira grabbed it and pulled out the contents. Inside was a single sheet of paper, covered in scrawled handwriting. Grandpa's script was bad enough at normal times, but this letter seemed to have been written in a terrible hurry, and his writing was worse than usual. Then there was the fact that a large portion of it was missing, having been eaten by the ... Greddish?

"Dear Margaret and Stefan," began the portion that remained. *"This is very urg ... Please find the map in my study, at the back of the second dra ... Bring it to me at once at the address giv ... It truly is a matter of life and d ... place is absolutely unbelievable ... Prester John's trail is prov ... wonders to be seen like you wouldn't bel ... wading through a bone-dry sea, only their heads show ... door quite literally in the exact middle of Nowhere ... a dust orchestra, complete with timpani and screeching sopranos, producing a song of de ... I MUST have it by Friday otherwise all will ... Exact coordinates of the Watchtower of the Secret*

Sands in the top ri ... Yours anxiously, Aloysius. P.S. Very dangerous, do NOT bring the childr ..."

The top right part of the letter, where the coordinates should have been, was missing entirely.

Mira shook her head. "He's in danger. We have to deliver his map to him. I wonder where he is?"

"It sounds amazing," said Marko. "He's seeing lots of incredible sights. Do you think he's in Hollywood?"

"Of course not," said his sister. But on further consideration, she decided that her brother might be thinking along the right lines. "It does sound a bit like a really incredible theme park. 'Wonders to be seen' and all that. Maybe it's Disneyland. Or Universal Studios."

"Or Legoland."

"We should have followed those weird messengers," said Mira.

"No, they said they weren't going back. But they could have told us where he was, maybe, and how to get there." Marko ran to the window to see if the men were still in sight. But the street was empty.

They reread the letter several times. Marko had seen the name Prester John before, in a history book about the journeys of a young explorer called Marco Polo. But the rest of the things mentioned in the letter—like the "dust orchestra" and the reference to "wading through a bone-dry sea"—well, none of it seemed to make much sense. But their grandfather, they knew, had once met the famous Chinese explorer Zheng He. Could he also have met Marco Polo?

The two children started going though their grandfather's desk drawers, looking for the map mentioned in the letter. In the room there was a lot of furniture, including two desks, several cabinets, and two dressers. All were stuffed with papers, boxes, and strange objects.

Ye Ye called himself a cultural anthropologist, whatever that was. It seemed to mean that he liked traveling to odd parts of the world and collecting strange artifacts—like the magic mirror, a circular metal plate from China that both reflected and filtered light, which was placed on his desk in the study.

They found a map at the back of the second drawer in his second desk.

Mira slipped it into her school backpack. "This must be it. We've got to get it to him by Friday. Perhaps he's been captured by someone and has promised to give him this in return for his life."

"But how do we deliver it if we don't know where he is?"

The girl scratched her chin. "Hmm ... I guess that does make it tricky. Any clues on the back of the envelope?"

There was nothing.

Mira sat down and thought. "Where can it be? A place of wonders, the most creative, imaginative, place in the world. Maybe it's the place where they make Japanese video games, which is probably in Tokyo? Or wherever most children's books are produced ... would that be in a publishing house in London? Or could it be Pixar Studios in America or something like that?"

There was another knock on the front door, but a much louder one this time. It was too assertive to be their previous visitors.

"Let's just be quiet and pretend we're out," said Mira.

"We're kids and it's nighttime. How can we be out?" said Marko, who had a nice line in logic.

His sister crept to the window. To her horror, she saw that their caller was Mr. Aldred. He knocked a second time.

Miranda slumped down on the floor and put her finger to her lips to tell her brother to be silent.

"Who is it?" he whispered.

"*Shhhhhh*. It's Mr. Aldred," she mouthed. "He knows we're living alone. He must have overheard us talking and guessed. He must have come to take us away and put us in an institution. It'll be horrible. Like in *Nicholas Nickleby* or *Oliver Twist*."

"It's all right," the boy said. "He can't get in. He doesn't have a key."

Just then, they heard a click: the unmistakable sound of a key entering a lock and being turned.

"Oh no," said Miranda. "We need to get out of here."

But the study had only one door … it led straight to the hall, where Mr. Aldred would now be standing. They could hear his voice from inside the house. "Hello? Anybody home?"

"Out the window?" Miranda asked.

"No, that way," said Marko, pointing to the small round window set high in the wall of the room.

"Are you crazy?" his sister asked.

He moved toward the door and switched off the room light.

The room was plunged into darkness … or should have been. But after the briefest of moments, their eyes adjusted to the fact that there was light from another source: it was evening, and a full moon was shining in the sky. It sent a pale, blue-white light into the room.

Marko pulled the magic mirror from his sister's backpack, and held it up to the circular window. The light shone through the thin metal filter, becoming harsher, and tinted with gold.

Mira said, "If the mirror is going to turn this into somewhere else, let's try and make sure it's the right place."

"Like where?"

"Like Disneyland. Or whatever theme park Grandpa is in."

She shut her eyes and started chanting: "Disneyland. Disneyland. Disneyland." She heard her brother join her.

"Disneyland. Disneyland. Disneyland. Wait. Florida? Or Epcot? Or Hong Kong? Or Tokyo?"

The gold light became increasingly bright. She closed her eyes. Now she could see red through her tightly closed eyelids.

She could hear the footsteps outside the room draw closer. "Faster," she whispered to no one in particular.

The light became more intense. Then there was a flash that hurt her eyes. The quality of air in the room changed. She suddenly felt hot. She took a step backward, but the floor seemed to shift under her feet. She fell down, landing on a yielding surface, like the soft, powdery sand you find above the tide line on a beach.

A Whole Lot of Nothing

Marko slowly opened his eyes. The light was so bright that he closed them again.

"You idiot," he heard his sister say. "This isn't Disneyland."

The boy didn't reply. He picked up some of the hot sand on which they sat and let it flow through his fingers. His sister had spoken the truth, although he couldn't see why this was his fault, other than the fact that he had been holding the mirror.

He gradually opened his eyes again and looked around. This sure wasn't Disneyland, or any kind of theme park. Instead of arriving at one of the most crowded, futuristic, entertainment-oriented spots on Earth, they had arrived at the opposite. They appeared to be in the middle of a desert, probably unchanged for centuries or millennia. A totally deserted desert, if such a thought had any value.

They were sitting close to the top of a sand dune, slightly on the leeward side. For as far as they could see in every direction, there was nothing. No people, no trees, no buildings, no signs of life. Just endless giant hills of sand.

The heat was intense. Marko could feel his hair getting hot. Within seconds, he felt his skin become slick and sweaty. He sat in thoughtful silence, knowing that his sister would do more than enough talking for both of them.

"We're gonna die," she whined. "We're in the desert with no food or water or people, and we're gonna die. Wait. Unless this is a hallucination. If you die in a hallucination, do you die in real life too? Ms. Modi reckons we have hallucinations because of all the sugar."

Marko didn't respond to her panic. This was not because he was brave, but because he was good at distracting himself. Whenever anything odd happened, he tried to avoid letting it scare him by thinking instead about what he could learn from it. The fact that the magic mirror had somehow made their grandfather's study, which was maybe six meters square, look and feel like a vast desert, stretching to the horizon … well, that was kind of cool. Could Ye Ye perhaps license the mechanism of the mirror to an entertainment company? Perhaps Nintendo, which could mass-produce them, sell them in time for Christmas?

Or perhaps this was a hallucination, like his sister had said. Again, he reached down and picked up some hot sand, letting it slip through his fingers. It seemed too real, too vivid, too tactile, to be a product of his imagination.

Carrying this thought further, he reflected on the fact that dreams normally focused on just sight, sound, and emotion. You could see and hear things, and you felt happy or worried or scared or excited. But this was different. All the senses were overloaded here. As well as seeing and hearing things, he could touch the sand, he could taste something burning in the air, and he could smell something salty in it, too.

Could there be other explanations? He'd seen movies of people going inside computer games—immersive virtual reality, they called it. Perhaps the magic mirror was not a light filter at all, but a projector. You held it up to the light, and it projected a sort of virtual reality world around you.

But then how come he had lowered the mirror to his lap, yet could still see the virtual world projected all around him? Further investigation was needed.

Marko rose to his feet. "Come on," he said.

"Where are we going?"

"I don't know. But we have to go somewhere. We can't just sit here until we are fried and dead."

"Why not?"

Marko wisely decided not to answer this question but merely walked toward the top of the dune. It was hard going—with each step, his feet sank into the sand and slid backward.

He sensed, rather than heard, his sister following.

"Why are we going in this direction?" she asked. "What makes it better than any other direction?"

"Nothing," he said. "But if we get to the top of the tallest dune we can at least see farther."

"If we get to the top of a dune, we'll be closer to the sun and we'll die of heatstroke."

"The sun is 92.96 million miles away. If we get to the top of this dune, we will be 92.96 million miles minus 30 feet away from the sun. I don't think it'll make a huge difference."

At the top of the dune, they looked down to see more nothing—miles of it, stretching to the horizon. In every direction.

"There's nothing here. We're going to die," Mira said.

"Wait, look!" Marko pointed to a tiny dot moving in the distance. "People."

A distant gray spot, when studied, seemed to be a tiny clump of individuals walking steadily in a trough between two large dunes.

Mira pointed in a different direction. "I can see something over there. Maybe another person, or a tree or something."

So there was life in the desert.

* * *

An hour later, Mira Lee and her brother were walking in the burning heat along a sort of path that seemed to wind between various dunes, and occasionally up and over small ones. Sometimes the path would disappear entirely, and they had to look carefully for signs of where it could be seen again.

Soon she noticed people in the distance ahead of them, and more people behind, so they guessed that they were going in the right direction. There must be something ahead.

After another ten minutes, she demanded they stop. "I need a drink. I need somewhere to sit. I need a restaurant. I need air-conditioning."

She sat down miserably on the sand, and her brother sat next to her.

They had barely rested three minutes when she heard something. Was that music? She turned her head to one side. "Listen. Can you hear that?"

Marko lifted his head. "Hear what?"

"Drumming. A band." She stood up. "It's coming from that direction. Ahead of us."

The sound was a low rumble, louder now, and unmistakable. "Are you sure it's drums?" the boy asked. "It sounds like thunder."

"It has a rhythm to it," the girl replied.

After holding her breath to listen harder, she realized that the drumming had some sort of pounding beat, like people banging huge African drums, or beating on timpani drums in an orchestra.

But then she noticed that the people walking in front of them, heading toward the music, had stopped. They had abruptly turned 180 degrees and were heading back the way they had come—moving swiftly toward the children.

Marko had apparently seen it, too. "Could the music be dangerous?" he asked.

"Of course not, that's dumb," said Mira, rising and moving forward.

Music of the Sands

Miranda and her brother marched steadily toward the drumming sound as the group of three adults in front of them fled from it.

As they came face to face, the trio, covered head to toe in robelike garments, barked at the two youngsters in a language they could not understand, and then hurried past.

"I think we should go with them," said Marko urgently. "They're warning us. The drummers may be bad guys, maybe soldiers or something."

"No, let's go to the source of the music," Mira replied, marching forward along the path. "It's not soldiers, I'm sure. Listen."

She was drawn not by the drumming itself but by another sound that she could hear—a female vocalist of some sort. There was a melodious wailing noise floating over the top of the thuds. At least one woman singing, maybe two or three.

"There's somebody there, someone singing, a girl," she said. Someone was producing a rather haunting sound, like you might hear on a soundtrack for a movie set in a desolate crag on an island off the Scottish coast or something. It reminded her of the theme from *Titanic*. The thought of Celine Dion singing, and Leonardo DiCaprio on a cruise ship, made her feet move faster.

The path led them around the side of a dune, and they saw more people hurrying toward them.

Her brother was becoming increasingly anxious. "Everyone's going in the opposite direction," he said. "I think we should turn around."

"They just don't like music," said Mira, who could be stubborn when she got an idea into her head. "I want to see who's singing."

The haunting sound was mesmerizing. It sounded like a mermaid or something, she decided. Didn't mermaids sing? But they were in a desert, so how could it be a mermaid? Maybe the mermaid was lost, and because of all the sand, thought she was on a really, really big beach. Perhaps she was crying to summon help.

As they topped a small dune and passed yet another band of people going in the opposite direction, Miranda could sense that Marko had stopped.

She turned to find him standing on the path, sixty feet behind her. "I think we should turn back," he said, more sternly this time.

"I'm going on. You decide whether to come with me or not," his sister said. She resumed her trek. After a moment, she noticed that he was still following her. She knew he would—he was too timid a boy to leave her side.

"OK, we stick together," he grumbled, "but if we die, it's your fault, right?"

"Right," she said. Everything was always her fault, anyway.

A further five or six minutes of walking led to a subtle change in the situation. The singing and drumming were louder, and seemed to be even shaking the sand. But there was a change in the air, too. A gusty wind was blowing, and the air was dusty, sending grit into their eyes.

Mira walked with her head down, trying to keep the grains of sand from stinging her face.

Marko looked up. "Stop," he said. "Look. There, ahead."

"Can you see her?" said Miranda, looking up and shielding her eyes to look toward the horizon.

"There," said Marko, "on the horizon—a black cloud."

Rubbing sand and sweat out of her eyes, Mira realized she could see something. But it was not really a black cloud. It was more like a line—a long, thin line, as if someone had drawn something on the horizon with a marker pen.

The black line grew thicker at a steady speed. How odd. What could it be? "It's some sort of sandstorm and it's coming toward us, fast," said Marko.

The wind rose quickly. Now it tore the tops of the dunes into wispy plumes of sand spiraling upward. The sky started to darken. The noise of drumming became louder. It sounded like the hooves of a thousand horses.

The children turned. It was clear they had to escape from it. But they were disoriented. "Which way?" Mira shouted. Suddenly she couldn't see her brother at all. "Marko? Marko! Where are you?"

There was no answer. Then his voice, as if from a distance: "I'm here. Where are you?"

Visibility vanished. And now the dark part of the storm was just seconds away from them. It started to push her around like a thousand hands.

Mira felt herself losing her balance—it was impossible to stay upright in the gale. But before she reached the ground, something powerful slammed into her with the force of a fast-moving vehicle.

* * *

Mira expected to find herself tumbling through the air, but instead she found herself scooped up and held tightly. If she had been snatched by the storm, it had a remarkably human-like arm. The sound of a herd of horses had been surmounted by the noise of a single animal's hooves, thundering just below her.

She'd been picked up by someone. She realized that a horseman had appeared out of nowhere and grabbed her, whipping her up and away from the black dust storm. Had her brother been snatched, too?

"Marko?" she screamed. "Marko!"

She could hear no response. Whoever was holding her continued to gallop. She opened her eyes the tiniest crack, but a painful blast of sand made her shut them again.

The person holding her barked something in a language she didn't understand. Mira held on tightly to the rider.

They galloped along the path for a long time, maybe eight or nine minutes, and she felt the horse turning at least twice, apparently threading its way along the paths between the larger dunes.

Once the wind dropped slightly and the rider slowed, Mira opened her eyes.

She was being carried by a man wrapped in layers of robes. A second rider behind was holding on to Marko.

"Thank you," she said. "Thank you."

As the horses slowed down to a stop, the man holding her shouted at her. He looked angry and his indecipherable words clearly expressed fury.

The other man said nothing as he held Marko with his left arm, while he guided his horse with his right hand.

As they turned downward into a steep-sided valley of dunes, the wind dropped further. The animals slowed, and the children were dropped to the ground with a bump.

"Ow," said Mira. "That hurt."

"They just saved our lives," Marko said. "Stop complaining."

One of the men got off his horse and walked over to the children, still scolding them in a language they couldn't understand.

"Can you speak English?" Marko asked.

The man stopped speaking. He looked to his friend. The other man, the one who had not spoken, strode over to them.

"Who you?" he said, his voice low. "Inglis?"

"Yes," said Mira. "We were going toward the sound of the drums." She mimed the movements of a drummer. "*Bang bang bang*. Drums, you know? And we could hear a singer? Singing?"

The man nodded. "Singing sands. Very danger. Go. Stay away." He pointed to his right, to a small path that wound between two dunes. Presumably that was the way to safety.

"Many way to die in desert," he said. "Many reason to stay away."

"Yeah, I guess," said Mira.

"Yesterday we found forty dead," he continued. "Men, women, children."

"Killed by the sand?"

He stared at them and ran his finger across his neck. "Throat cut," he said. "The hordes are restless."

Hordes of what? Mira didn't know what to say. "Ah, thank you for that information," she eventually replied.

As they dusted themselves off and walked along the path the men had showed them, she moved closer to her brother. She found herself grinning, and not just because of their narrow escape.

"That was a bit grim, but it's actually good news," she said.

"That we survived?"

"That too. But think what this means. We're not in the wrong place after all," she said. "We're in the right place. Grandpa's letter talked about the orchestra of dust, remember? That black wind that made a noise like drummers and people singing. That was the orchestra of dust. It's a sign. We're on our way to save him."

Marko nodded. "Maybe," he said.

As they strode onward, evening started to fall.

A Vision in the Night

They walked for about thirty-five minutes before they saw lights in the distance. Dusk was falling fast. The heat of the desert had vanished, and the temperature was dropping steadily. It became cool, almost pleasant.

Marko realized that this would probably be a brief interlude, as the temperature was on its way from way too hot to way too cold. He'd done enough reading about deserts to know they were places of uncomfortable extremes.

"We need to find somewhere to stay," he said to Mira, as they approached a cluster of homes, mostly one story tall.

"Do you think they have hotels here?" she asked. "I don't mean like big flashy ones with limousines out front, but little ones, or a YMCA."

"Hotels? What do we pay with? We don't have any money."

"Couldn't they charge it to our parents?" she said.

He thought for a moment. "I guess they could if we had our parents' credit card numbers. Next time we better ask for them."

Marko looked at the houses, which were basically made out of mud with thatched roofs. He remembered a book in school in which these types of building were called wattle and daub: they had wooden frameworks on which fast-drying mud was slapped and then baked hard by the sun.

"You know, I don't think they'll accept credit cards here," he said.

"What makes you say that?"

"I don't think we're in today, if you know what I mean. The last time the magic mirror dropped us into a dream, we were in the year 1400 or something, remember? I think the same thing may have happened again."

As they peered at the people in the houses, they got a lot of stares back.

Mira took offense. "What's wrong with everyone? Hasn't anyone seen board shorts before?"

Marko said, "I don't think they have. There are no cars, no roads, and no planes have flown overhead. Also, there are no TV antennae on any of the buildings."

"No TV?" said Mira, looking at the roof line. "Wow. Amazing. We must be way back in the past. Perhaps we can meet Zheng He again? So, what do we do now?"

Although Mira was the older sibling, and she rarely let Marko forget it, she often turned to him for help in solving complex problems. Marko was a reader. He read constantly, and knew all sorts of unlikely things that helped them out of scrapes. It seemed to her that her brother remembered every single thing he had ever read.

"Where are we going to sleep? It'll be dark soon. Any ideas?"

"A piece of thick cloth spread over a bundle of hay can make a comfortable bed," he said. "I read it somewhere."

Within minutes the light had all but disappeared. They borrowed some robes that were hanging out to dry and then headed to a part of town where camels were kept.

There were guards there, so they headed back the way they came. Although they had never been to this town, it was small, just a place where three roads met, and within minutes they knew it quite well. Then they found a small path leading to smaller dwellings, including one that looked like the outhouse of a small farm. The barnlike structure had a damaged wall through which the two kids could easily sneak. Inside they found animals and hay. "Ew, sleeping in a stinky animal stable, this is definitely not cool," said Mira.

"Just think like it's Christmas and you're sleeping in a manger ...," said Marko.

Although she didn't like to admit it, the thought actually did make her feel better. "Marko," she said, as they tried to get comfortable. "I remember hearing that it gets really cold in the desert at night. After boiling to death during the day, do you think we might freeze to death tonight?"

"Maybe," he replied. "But since animals are kept here, probably we'll be OK. These people wouldn't want their animals to die. So I think we should be fine."

Ten minutes later they were fast asleep, half-buried in a pile of hay. Whatever book Marko had remembered had been right. A thick blanket on a bed of hay really was surprisingly comfortable.

* * *

Miranda woke in the middle of the night. Someone had called her name. Or had it been a dream? She opened her eyes and looked around. "Mira," said a voice again.

It was dark except for a green glow in one corner of the room. She crawled over to it. The light seemed to be coming from her backpack. There must be a flashlight or something inside. It would help her see whoever was calling her.

Opening the bag, she realized that it was the magic mirror that was glowing. The strange, plate-shaped disk with the wavy edges still had not released all its secrets. An ancient Chinese artifact, it seemed to work in various ways. You could polish it and look at your reflection in the surface. You could hold it up to the light and use it as a filter. Or you could look into it, almost as if it was a portal.

And that's what she found herself doing. She gazed into the mirror, past the reflection of herself, into the gentle green light that shone from somewhere inside.

She saw nothing clearly. But there were indistinct lines and shapes, and something seemed to be moving. "Mira," whispered the voice from inside. And then some of the lines moved together—she realized that eyes had blinked.

"Who are you? Where are you?"

"On the other side," said the voice. "I have important information for you. Can you see me clearly? Look harder. Come closer."

She leaned close to the mirror's surface and squinted, trying to focus past her reflection. She had a sense of a deep space inside, as if she was looking into a three-dimensional chamber, but through a glass smeared with dust or grease. Someone inside was speaking to her, but she could not see them well. The figure leaned into the frame from the left-hand side, and she could just see an ear and one green eye.

"I can't see you properly," she said. "Can you stand in the middle?"

"Seeing me is not important," said the breathy voice. "Seeing what I have to show you is vital."

Fingertips appeared around the inside edges of the frame, and there was movement in the space. The figure carried his side of the mirror, moving it toward the back of the room.

She saw now that it was a large chamber. On a shelf behind her, she saw many tall, thin, shiny objects. As one in particular came into focus, she saw that it was a large hourglass.

"Who are you, and why are you showing me this?"

"Because you need to see it."

"The hourglass? Why does the sand glow? Is it radioactive?"

"They are not sand grains. They are lives."

"Ew, you mean there are millions of tiny things in there, like bugs or something?"

"No. They are your grandfather's lives."

Sand moved slowly from the upper chamber of the glass into the narrow hole below—but then disappeared. The bottom half of the hourglass was empty.

"Lives? Is it like reincarnation or something?"

The voice spoke softly, like a breeze. "No. Each grain in the higher part is a life he could lead, choices he could make: possibilities, if you like. When a person is born, there are an almost limitless number of lives ahead of him, choices he could make, paths to follow, people to meet. But as one gets older, the number falls continuously. If a person is very old, or very sick, or in grave danger of some sort, the number of possibilities falls dramatically."

She stared at the glass.

The voice continued: "Your grandfather started life with a huge number of possible lives ahead of him, as indeed do all human beings. But he has lived a long time, and the number has fallen dramatically."

She realized that there was very little sand in the top half. "How come people don't know about this? Isn't it kind of important? Shouldn't people be told?" She realized that she could see a rough reflection of the speaker in the hour glass. He was tall and appeared to be dressed in white.

"People do know about this," the voice breathed. "But it tends to be in their subconscious rather than their conscious minds. Some young people don't get up until half the day is gone, for they know without consciously considering it that they have seemingly limitless futures in front of them. Old people know that the number of lives they can choose from has diminished dramatically. They rise early to make the most of each day. Again, they may never think directly about this, but they are aware of it, nonetheless. Indeed, it drives them."

"Who are you, and why are you showing me this?"

"I am a guardian."

"Guardian? Like a guardian angel?"

"I am your grandfather's guardian. We are not supposed to give you such information directly, so I must ask you to keep my presence secret. But I have contacted you because he is in grave danger. I need you to realize that only you can save him."

"If you're his guardian angel, can't you save him? Isn't that your job?"

"I work using human hands," the voice said. "I am sending someone to save him, by delivering the map he needs. I am sending you. Tomorrow you must go into the desert. That is all I have to tell you at the moment."

The image started to fade.

"Wait. Can I talk to you again?"

"I will talk to you from time to time, but only at night. During the day, the light from your world is too bright, and hurts me."

The image faded completely. Mira found herself looking only at the reflection of her own face. And then the green light disappeared too, and she was sitting in the dark holding a piece of metal.

She put the magic mirror back into the bag, and crawled to her corner of the hay bales. She imagined that she would lie awake all night, thinking about what she had been told.

But she was exhausted and soon fell into a troubled sleep.

Searching for Help

The next morning, searing heat followed the arrival of dawn, with barely five minutes' grace. As soon as daylight crept into the barn, the temperature rose steadily.

But it remained quiet. There were some snuffling noises from two small horses, the only occupants of the barn, and the buzz of insects from outside.

Miranda woke with a start and sat up. She shook her brother awake, and said: "We need to make a move, find Grandpa. We've only got a few days to find him. We need to go into the desert today."

"What happened? Did you have a dream or something?"

She didn't answer. Had it been a dream? Or were they having a dream right now? Did that make it a dream within a dream? But whatever had happened, she had been given information that made sense. Grandpa needed the map. They needed to get it to him as soon as they could.

They rose and sneaked out of the crack in the wall. At a drinking trough for horses, they splashed water on their faces. Then they headed to the crowded part of town.

"I'll take charge now," said Miranda. "The first thing we need is some information. We need some adult help. We had better make friends with someone who knows the desert and can guide us to where we need to go. In a place like this, you probably can't just go to the tourist information booth, or the police station. They probably don't have such things."

This turned out to be true. The town was small, and within half an hour, they had been around all its streets twice over. There didn't seem to be any organization they could call on for help. For a start, no one spoke a word of English. Their few attempts to talk to people led to bafflement on both sides. And they were getting hungry.

"Did you ever read a book about a situation like this?" Miranda asked.

Marko thought for a moment. "About people who were lost and hungry with no money? Hmm, let me think. In *Jane Eyre*, there's a bit where she's wandering around with no food or shelter. But she found help eventually. That was in England, I guess."

"Yeah, she had it easy. She was in a place where people spoke the same language she did. Perhaps the first thing we need to do is find someone who speaks English."

"How do we do that?"

"Easy, just shout something in English and see who turns around," Miranda said. "You do it. Boys are more shouty than girls."

"I don't think 'shouty' is a word."

"Just do it."

"OK, what do I shout?"

"I don't know, any English shout."

Marko thought for a moment. "I can't think of anything. How about 'Yabba-dabba-doo!'?"

"That's not English."

"Well, what is it?"

"It's American. It's an American TV show."

"I don't think it's American. American isn't a language."

"OK, well it's Caveman. Or Flintstone. Whatever, it's not English."

"Well, you think of something to shout then."

"I can't think of anything. What do people shout when they do shout things, like at sports matches and things?"

Marko thought about the last time he had watched soccer on television, which had been a year ago. "They sing: 'Here we go, here we go, here we go.'"

"That's a good idea. Come on, let's go where we can be heard."

Mira led him up a rickety staircase to a rooftop on one of the few two-story buildings. It projected out over the town's marketplace, where traders were already exchanging vegetables and other goods. They started singing: "Here we go, here we go, here we go."

There was no response, so they decided to sing something else. Mira took the lead with a silly song she used to sing in the playground: "On top of spaghetti, all covered with cheese, I lost my poor meatball ... it fell on my knees."

They soon had several people looking up at them. Most of them smiled and laughed at the sound of two children singing what to them was gibberish at the top of their voices.

"Do you think anyone understands what we're saying?" Mira said, after several repeats of the spaghetti song. "It doesn't look like they do. Maybe no one here speaks English. We may have to learn desert language."

She followed his finger. Two men seemed to be listening to what they were singing. "Sing it again. Louder."

"On top of spaghetti, all covered in cheese, I lost my poor meatball …"

"They *do* understand. They're discussing us."

They waved at the two men and then scrambled down the stairs to meet them.

* * *

The two men met them at the corner of the market. One was pale-skinned, looked European, and was maybe seventeen or eighteen years old. The other was dark-skinned with heavy black facial hair. He reminded Mira of Daddy's friend Jashan—so maybe he was from India or Sri Lanka or somewhere like that.

"You speak English?" he asked, his head cocked to one side in curiosity.

"Yes, and we're looking for people who do too. That's why we were singing," Mira said.

"Your parents are where?"

"Our guardian is our grandfather just now. But we've lost him. In the desert. We have to find him soon. Can you help us?"

The pale-skinned young man spoke. "We can give you some advice, but I think you should not travel with us. We are going on a very high-risk journey. It's not safe for children." He had a European accent of some sort. *Eet's not safe for cheeldren.*

"But you have to take us," Mira said. "We need to get into the desert to find him."

The young man shook his head. "It's going to be hard enough keeping ourselves alive. We don't want to have to worry about you two as well. I am so sorry. If we find your grandfather, we can give him a message."

"Please, it's our only hope," she said.

The dark man pulled two pieces of fruit out of his bag and handed them to the children. "We're sorry we cannot help you. Please take these, for your breakfast."

Mira folded her arms crossly. "If you don't let us go with you, we'll go by ourselves."

"That would be your decision," said the young European man, now rather cross.

Marko accepted the fruit gratefully and decided to try another line of argument. "Maybe we can help each other. You're also travelers, right? What are you looking for?"

"Never mind," said the man with the beard. "What you need is to find someone to look after you. The Taklamakan is no place for children."

The two men turned and walked away.

Marko shouted after them. "Our grandfather went in search of Prester John. Do you know where we can find him?"

The young European man stopped. He turned. "What did you say?"

"Our grandfather went to find Prester John," said Marko. "He found lots of amazing sights. He sent us a letter asking us to join him. He's probably found him by now."

The two men walked back to the children, their expression suddenly serious. The bearded man said, "Tell us what you know."

"I'll do the talking." said Mira. "We have lots of really, really interesting information. Our grandfather gave us lots of clues about where to find Prester John and about the wonders we'll see on the way. It's a long story. We'll tell you on the road."

The older man looked at them with puzzlement. "Truly," he said, "I have never seen such strange children as you. Your grandfather, you say, has gone into the desert and written a letter to ask you to join him? Is he knowledgeable about the desert, and what can be found there?" He looked from one child to the other.

"Oh yes, he knows everyone," said Miranda, confidently. "Anyone who's anyone in the desert, he knows him."

"Has he mentioned a man named Wang Han? Or Toghrul?"

"I don't think so," said Marko.

"Yes, probably," said Mira, kicking her brother in the shin, "but maybe under a different name."

The man smiled. "My name is Ashok. I am a desert tracker. I seek a man named Wang Han. He comes from the family of the Great Khan."

"Genghis Khan?" asked Marko. "Or Kublai Khan?"

Ashok's eyes widened. He looked at the youngsters and then glanced at his partner. "You children are well educated."

"I had to do the poem for homework last year," Mira said. "Marko did it this year. 'In Xanadu did Kublai Khan a stately pleasure-dome decree ...'"

"You know about Xanadu?"

"Oh yes," said Mira, trying to sound nonchalant. "My grandfather goes there all the time. It's like his home away from home."

The younger man stepped forward. His hostility had vanished and now his face was bright. He was suddenly very interested in them. "You mentioned Prester John. What do you know about this man?"

"Not much," said Marko. "Except that Grandpa mentioned him in his letter. He's probably hanging out with him. Anyway, he's mentioned in one of my history books, I think, although I don't remember much about him. Was he the guy who was king of a kingdom but nobody knew where it was? He had lots of treasure?"

Marko remembered that the Venetian explorer Marco Polo had traveled around Asia looking for strange and magical sights. He'd looked for famous people too—

Prester John was one of them. Could this young man be the famous traveler? He looked too young, just a teenager.

The two men stared at each other, and then looked back at the children.

"Who has taught you such things?" said Ashok.

"Er, I read a lot. My family has a lot of books, and I spend a lot of time in the school library, reading on the Internet, that sort of thing."

"He's a reader," agreed Mira. "Addicted. Reads everything. Cereal boxes at the table. The other kids say it's uncool, but I say it's way cool."

The two men stepped away to talk. After less than three minutes, they turned back to the children. "You may come with us," the European man said. "You may be useful to us. We will share food and provisions with you. You share information with us. We would like to meet this grandfather of yours."

"Sure," said Mira. She turned to the younger man and gave him a smile. "And what's your name?"

The young man smiled and held out his hand. His grin was infectious and his eyes twinkled. "I am Marco Polo Emilione of Venice, Italy. You can call me Emil."

"Pleased to meet you, Emil," said Mira and was surprised when her brother leaned forward eagerly, holding out his hand.

"So you are Marco Polo!" said the boy. He added, "My name's Marko, too. Although I spell mine with a *K*."

Into the Heat

Two hours later, Miranda was convinced that once
again she had made a huge mistake.

They had gone back into the desert. It was hot and
miserable and once more she felt like they were going
to die.

The small party of travelers had left almost
immediately, anxious to get to their first stop before
the sun was too high in the sky. That meant two hours
of travel in a morning that was already way too hot.
After that, they would camp through the hottest part
of the day and then set off again as the sun fell to the
horizon.

We're going to die, Mira thought again. Why did we volunteer for this? Everything I do seems to be a huge mistake. But then she forced herself to look on the bright side. The men had four camels, which meant that the two kids did not have to walk. Instead, they could doze fitfully in the searing heat, white robes covering their heads, as they were carried along by the plodding beasts.

And she had been given encouragement by the fact that the young European man they found might be an actual celebrity. Her brother had said that he could be the famous traveler Marco Polo. If this was true, then she really did have something majorly cool to write in her diary when she got back.

Ashok rode in front, Emil behind, and the two children sat on the third camel, with a fourth, carrying supplies, bringing up the rear.

Staying on a camel was surprisingly hard work, she decided. Unlike cars and horses, which go in a straight line, camels were more like elephants. Their whole bodies tilted slightly to one side or the other with each step they took. They kind of rolled continuously from left to right and back again.

And sleeping on them was tough, she realized. The trouble was that sleep tended to creep around one's body. Your legs went to sleep first, twitching and then becoming dead weights. Then your body became still. Then your head drifted away into a muddle of thoughts that were the seeds of dreams. But as your head floated away, the sleep crept down your arms and tried to loosen your fingers from their death grip on the handles that held you on your mount. That's when you had to jerk yourself awake, to make sure you didn't let go and fall off.

Marko seemed to have no problems, leaning on her and snoring. Normally, she would have shaken him off, but this time, she let him snore on her shoulder. He had helped a lot on this journey, even if he was stupid and annoying occasionally—well, pretty much all the time. For instance, he thought "Yabba-dabba-doo!" was an English phrase. Who could believe that?

* * *

As the sun climbed higher, they reached their first stop, a village with a hard-to-pronounce name that meant "wall," according to Ashok. Despite this, it had no wall around it.

"It marks the point where the desert becomes impenetrable," the desert tracker said, as they sat in a relatively cool, dark hall in a white building, sipping coconut water. "This is the point where people turn back. It's a sort of symbolic barrier, an invisible one. It's the last stop for most travelers. They turn west from here, skirting the edge of the desert."

"But you said it was our first stop," Mira said. "For us, it's the first stop. We're going into the heart of the Taklamakan."

"*Makan* means 'eat' in some languages," said Miranda, thinking of her Singaporean and Malaysian schoolmates.

"It's different here," said Ashok. "*Taklamakan* is a local phrase meaning 'abandoned place.' Some people translate the name to mean 'place of death.'"

The explanation sent a shiver up her spine.

"Do we have to go in? Can't we just talk to the locals, and find out what information we need from them? Maybe find a shortcut to the other side, or go round the edge or ..." She was about to suggest that they hire a helicopter, but then decided not to mention it.

She turned to the younger man, who was pretty good-looking, she decided. "Excuse me, Emil, what year is this?"

"It is the year of our Lord 1273," he said. "For children who know so much about esoteric things, it surprises me that you know so little about ordinary things."

Mira bridled at being referred to as a child, but said nothing.

Ashok spoke, standing up as he did so. "Enough talk. Now it is important that we all get some sleep. We have a long distance to cover when the sun comes off its zenith. We need to be well rested. The path ahead is known as the Road of No Return. It will not be an easy journey."

Miranda and Marko were given a pair of blankets and sent to a corner of the room.

"No way am I going to sleep in this heat," said Miranda. Ten minutes later, she was snoring.

* * *

They were woken four or five hours later by the tracker. After spending almost an hour reloading the camels, they set off. The sun still burned fiercely in the sky, but they could see that it was on its way down to the horizon. Miranda guessed it was about four o'clock.

They plodded in silence on the first part of the second leg of the journey, but after an hour or so, the heat started to abate and everyone relaxed a bit.

Ashok turned out to be a great storyteller. He told them that he had started exploring when he heard the story of Xuanzang, a Chinese monk who had traveled to India to find the Buddhist scriptures and take them back to China. The Chinese Buddhist scriptures were not the same as those in India, and Xuanzang was anxious that China should have a complete collection.

"It happened more than 400 years ago," he said. "Then I got the idea of traveling north into China and doing the same thing in reverse: finding ancient texts from China and bringing them back to India."

"So you are on your way to China?" said Mira. "They have this really cool food there called noodles. You're gonna love it."

Ashok smiled. "Tell Marco Polo Emilione," he chuckled. "He's a great one for trying new cuisines."

Emil laughed, and then Ashok continued his tale. He explained that there were some remarkable lost writings in this part of the world, including the early drafts of a book called *The Secret History of the Mongols*, compiled after the death of the great king known as Genghis Khan. "This man is responsible for the biggest kingdom in creation," he said. "It is bigger than the lands of the entire Roman Empire, bigger than the lands of Alexander the Great, bigger than the lands of the Indian emperor Chandragupta Maurya. What a story he must have."

"He must have been a very great warrior," said Emil.

"True, but there is something else unusual about him. Although he is a violent man and a shamanist and has his own witch doctors to guide his sacrifices to the many gods in which he believes, at the same time, he was very tolerant of other men's gods. Many years ago, he gathered twenty men around himself to make an agreement called the Baljuna Covenant. The men came from nine tribes, including the tribes of the Christ, the Buddha, and the Prophet—all lived in peace together."

Mira listened with rapt attention as Ashok told the story of the warrior king and his family who conquered most of Asia, and united the many parts of China into one country, with its headquarters at Beijing.

But she was most entranced to hear about Genghis Khan's daughter-in-law, whose name was Beki. She interrupted Ashok. "Wait. Becky? As in Rebecca? That's a name we use a lot in the place where we come from. One of my best friends at school is called Becky. It seems weird to hear of an ancient princess called Becky."

Ashok laughed. "Not so ancient, her son is the current emperor of China. The princess's name was Sorghaghtani Beki. She was a Christian and very influential, and so the kingdom has an interesting mix of characteristics: strength from the warrior king, gentleness from the religions gathered there. Her son is named Kublai Khan."

Ashok told the children that Genghis Khan's violence had made him millions of enemies—including some of his former friends. "An old warlord, Wang Khan, was at one time Genghis's godfather, but they had a bitter disagreement, and fought over the kingdom. Wang Khan was also Sorghaghtani Beki's beloved uncle, and known by many names, including Wang Han, Toghrul, Ong Khan, and others."

"You're looking for this guy?" asked Marko.

Ashok nodded. "Legend has it that he was accidentally killed by his own men after fleeing from a battle his side was losing. Certainly he disappeared from view many years ago. But other legends say that he put out the story that he was dead so that he could retreat from the world with some treasures that had been accumulated—including, some even say, the Fountain of Youth and, I hope, a few rare texts."

"Where is he hiding?" Mira asked.

"At the end of the Road of No Return."

Emil's Story

A s they set off once more, into the face of the setting sun, a spectacular blue-pink-orange universe above them, Ashok explained how people survived in the desert when they had run out of water. "You dig for a well—even here in the driest place on Earth there is water not far away."

Marko was fascinated, seeing an opportunity to add to his mental storehouse of geography and weather facts. "How do you know where the water will be? There aren't any signposts."

"If there are trees, we dig there. If not, we find a spot exactly in the middle of two particular types of dunes. Then we dig straight down. Usually, when we get to a depth equivalent to the height of a man, we find the ground is damp. We leave the hole and wait. After a while, a little brackish water can be found at the bottom. Sometimes we leave it all night, and wake up the next morning to find a hand's depth of water at the bottom."

"Does it always work?"

The explorer shook his head. "This is dangerous work. I know of cases where people have exhausted themselves digging, only to find the ground dry because they have chosen the wrong spot. When one is too dehydrated to dig another hole, death is inevitable."

Marko bit his lip. The thought chilled him. One mistake could mean the end.

As they traveled into the gathering darkness, it was Emil's turn to tell his story. He was a highly observant young man, and threw lots of detail into his descriptions.

"When I was six, my father and his brother disappeared, having gone on a journey," he said in his distinctive, musical accent. "Many men in my home went on journeys to do business—we lived in a small port town called Venice that was known as the floating city. The streets themselves are rivers, and we traveled to school every day by boat, not by foot or by horse carriage. It's a marvelous place in itself—you must come and visit. Anyway, many traders travel out of the city, but most come back after a day or a week or a month, bearing contracts or orders for business deals from neighboring towns.

"But not my father and his brother. They went very far, traveling for many years. They sent back letters recounting amazing tales. Then one day they returned with strange objects and even stranger stories, about magical beasts and adventures they had in a land called Cathay.

"I listened to these tales and longed to go with them. They wanted to go back to the magical lands, because there were many things they had heard of that they had not yet seen, so many others things to collect and stories to confirm.

"Last year they decided to do the journey once more. I begged my guardians to let me go with them. And so, on my seventeenth birthday, we set off. That was nine months ago. It takes a year to go to Cathay from Venice, if you travel directly. But my father taught me something important. Leave much more time for your journey than you need, because then the journey can become part of the destination—wise words indeed."

Mira was curious. "So where are your father and your uncle? Did you lose them?"

"There is so much to see on the road ... even with the extra time we put into our schedule, so we made plans to split up and investigate things individually from time to time. When we reached this area, we went in three directions, with a plan to meet in six months. My father went due north. My uncle Matteo took a western route. And I went due east to see if I could find the tracks of Prester John."

Mira asked, "You weren't scared to go off on your own without them?"

"Of course not," he scoffed. He added, after a moment, "But I was glad to have Ashok to travel with. And travelers always meet interesting people on the road ... like you."

Mira found herself blushing.

They traveled until it was dark and cold, and the camels were reluctant to go any further. There they stopped and made a camp.

Mira and Marko once more slept the sleep of exhaustion.

* * *

After another day's trekking through a featureless desert, Mira began to despair.

"We haven't seen anything for ages," she told her brother. "Maybe we should tell the guys to turn back. There were some towns back near where we started, but here, there's just nothing."

"Nothing is what we want," Marko replied. "We're looking for a place called Nowhere, remember? In the letter, Grandpa said we'd find the door in the desert, right in the middle of it."

Emil had been taking notes throughout the travels, but now had run out of things to write about. There are only so many ways to describe dunes.

Mira wondered why Marco Polo was using the name Emil. She decided to strike up a conversation with him. "You have three names. So, which is your family name and which is your personal name?"

"It's complicated," said Emil. "In the city where I was born, there are many families with the surname Polo, so we differentiate ourselves using different names, a middle name or a traditional family name. In Venice, my family is called Emilione. That's the official version. But our nickname for our clan is The Million. There are a lot of us, although not in reality a million. In my language, Italian, we say *Il Milione*, which sounds like Emilione. Thus my given name is Marco, my family name is Polo, and my nickname is Emil."

Marko interrupted. "Can you tell us more about Prester John?"

"Sure. For some years, there have been rumors of a magic kingdom in the East, run by a Christian king named Prester John. It is said to contain many wonderful treasures, including the Holy Grail, which is the cup used by Christ at the Last Supper. And there are other legends too, some of which are too fantastical to be true."

"So it could all be just made-up stories?" Marko asked.

Emil shook his head. "There are enough believable stories to persuade me that there is some sort of secret community out here. My father and uncle were skeptical. On their earlier travels to the East, they saw or heard nothing about such a king or kingdom. But when we met Ashok, and he told us of the Christian family of Genghis Khan, I realized that there really could be a hidden Christian kingdom in the Orient, somewhere in this region. That's when I was filled with the desire to find it."

* * *

In the early morning of the third day, they came across a grim sight—a scattered pile of white bones, gleaming in the early sunlight.

Marko gazed at them, looking for horns—if he saw horns, then he would know that they would be animal bones. *But if not* ... he didn't want to continue the thought. He remembered the words of the pair of horsemen who had saved them from the dust storm. There were killers in the sands.

His sister put into words the question in his mind, saying, "Hey, Ashok. Are those animal bones? Or people bones?"

He turned to her, "Let's just keep moving," he said.

His lack of a straight answer convinced Marko that he was better off not knowing the truth. He looked away from them.

Gazing in the opposite direction, he saw movement to their far left. "Over there," he said. "I can see people."

Ashok was already staring in that direction. "I recognize the headgear," he said, his voice cracking. "It looks like a rogue band of bandits from the Golden Horde. Keep moving, steadily and slowly. We don't want to attract their attention."

But it was too late. The group of horsemen had seen them. Worse, they soon started to move toward them.

And the numbers grew. When Marko had sighted them, he'd seen just three figures. But there were six people on horseback approaching now. They reached for their scabbards.

"I don't like this," Emil said. "They're getting out their weapons."

Marko raised his hands to his ears. He did not want to hear this. Next to him, he felt Miranda whimper and scrunch up her shoulders in fear.

Unable to help himself, he glanced to the left. The riders disappeared as they dipped into a sand valley for several seconds, and then they reappeared—now there were more than twenty of them, and their weapons glinted in the sunlight. They were heading straight for them, murder on their minds. "We're going to die," said Mira.

* * *

"There," said Ashok, pointing toward the sun. Marko followed his finger. There was something shimmering in the distance. It looked like a lake. And there were other objects just beyond it.

"Head for the lake town," the tracker shouted. "No, head for the southwest, follow me."

Emil added, "Go as fast as you can. It's going to be tough to outrun the horde."

But as they galloped after Ashok, Marko and Mira heard the drums again. It was curious, as it really sounded like someone banging timpani. There was a rhythm to it, and melodic notes that throbbed, rising and falling in volume. It was almost impossible to believe that the sound was created purely by sand.

Mira sounded the warning. "It's the orchestra of dust, my grandfather says in his letter."

"It's an orchestra of death," said Ashok. "Normally, we would avoid it, but this time it may just be our friend."

"We saw one earlier," Marko shouted. "It's horrible, dangerous."

But the tracker peered at the dark cloud floating toward them. "This is a small dust storm moving from the southwest to the east. I've seen these many times. We call them floating rivers. We can go straight through it—far safer to risk it than to let the horde get us. Indeed, it may scare the horde away. They have less experience in these quarters than I do."

"River? Is it wet?" Emil asked.

"No, but you'll see how it moves. These storms flow across the surface of the sand, a hand's width above the dune surface, and less than a man's height—like black water, but dry."

As they galloped toward it, the throbbing sound grew louder, the air turned gray, the sun disappeared, and soon the storm was upon them. They could see a low-lying cloud moving swiftly across the dunes.

Emil was amazed. "It is just as you say, Ashok, a river. It will flow around the bottoms of the camels' legs, I suppose. Will they still be able to walk?"

The tracker nodded. "It depends on how deep and how strong it is. Usually, it's not dangerous if you are on a camel and it's coming from the west. The only thing that would be bad is if the wind changed and it came from the east—those winds are much faster, and can turn the river of sand into a deep torrent, taller than a camel, taller than the tallest tree even."

As they thundered along away from the men behind them, Marko grabbed his sister's arm. "You know what this is, don't you?"

"What?"

"It's what Grandpa mentioned in his letter. Something about walking through a bone-dry sea?"

"Oh yes. Something about 'heads wading through a dry sea.'"

"If the dust river is three or five feet deep, you would only see people's heads."

"I guess it must be what he wrote about. Anyway, the guy says it isn't dangerous as long as the storm comes from the west."

"What about that one?"

"What one?"

"I can see a cloud coming from that direction. Look. That thin black line. See it?"

She peered in the direction of his finger. "Yeah, I see it, but who says that's from the east?"

"I do. That's the direction the sun rose."

She called out to the camel in front. "Ashok. Ashok!"

He turned to them and spoke rapidly, urgency in his voice, "There's a storm wind coming from the east, now. Two dust storms arriving at once—plus a band of villains on our tail. It's going to be too high for us to manage. Head for the oasis, the lake town, as fast as you can. Follow me."

He pointed due west, where there was the glimmer of water. They spurred their camels onward, heading for the lake on the horizon.

The tracker called again, "Go faster, faster. It's accelerating and we have a long way to go."

Mira bit her lower lip and held on for dear life. The dark clouds flew at them over the tops of the dunes, heading straight for them from two directions.

She looked back. The men chasing them had stopped moving, having spotted the clouds flying over the sand.

The darkness was approaching at high speed. There was no way they could outrun it. The dust river quickly reached them and was quickly lapping around the camel's knees. She could feel the abrasion from the flying sand scratching at her feet, and then moving up her body as the level rose.

It got higher and higher until her whole body felt battered by the sand, which was like a thousand tiny hammers striking at her. Then it reached her neck. Beside her, she could see Marko almost standing as he tried to keep his head above the level of flying sand.

She prayed for the wind to drop, but it just got louder, harder, and faster.

It reached her face and suddenly she couldn't breathe anymore. The stinging grains of sand whipped into her eyes and nostrils and mouth and ears.

Then she heard a scream in a foreign language. Ashok must have shrieked something as it reached his head too.

Suddenly she felt the camel drop. She tumbled off it into the depths of the raging river of killer sand.

The Middle of Nowhere

It was dark. It was loud. It was hot.

But she was alive. She found herself lying on the sand, her head flat against the ground. She could breathe again. She remembered that Ashok had said that the river of sand floated a hand's width above the surface of the ground. The shout that she had heard: it must have been the tracker giving a command to the camels to fall to ground level.

"Marko," she shouted. "You OK?"

"Fine," he said. "Down at this level you can breathe. But don't lift your head. I did, and I felt like the sand was trying to rip my ear off."

"Yes, better stay flat," said Ashok's voice calling from some distance ahead. "Move to your right so you are in the shade of the camel. His head will be flat on the ground. If you crawl up next to his body you should get a bit of shelter." They did as the tracker said and soon found themselves hunched up against the camel, which had laid itself flat on the sand.

"This is weird."

"You said it, sis."

"And smelly."

"Camels are."

"An adventure to remember."

"If we survive to remember it."

Emil called out somewhere from behind them, "You'll be fine. Just keep your heads down."

After twenty minutes, the sound changed in tone, moving from a low rumble to a lighter, higher sound, almost like a chorus of whistles. Then they felt the wind change, lightening in intensity and moving to the west.

They heard Emil shouting, "The wind's falling fast. Hopefully when the storm clears, we'll be close to the oasis."

It was another eleven or twelve minutes before the wind subsided enough for them to see clearly and rise to their feet.

"Which way is it?" Miranda asked, looking around. "I could sure do with a hotel right now. A warm shower, a blow-dryer for my hair, followed by room service bringing me french fries."

She spun around, peering in every direction. There was no sign of the lake they had seen, or the oasis or trees or anything else. "What happened? Did the storm blow the whole town away, lake and trees and all? And the horde. It's blown away the horde."

Ashok shook his head. "I'm sorry to have bad news. The lake must have been a mirage. Usually I can tell the difference, but I've never been to this part of the desert, and it looked so real. I can hardly believe it myself."

There was no denying the truth of what was all around them. There was no lake. The storm had caused some flattening of the dunes, and they could see a dry ocean of sand all the way to the horizon.

"We need to get moving again." He showed them how to get their camels back up and ready to move.

* * *

They trekked through most of the cool of the evening, and then took a break when it was cold and dark. Once more they slept well, exhausted by their adventures.

The next morning, they rose early and traveled for two hours.

"Why would Wang Han or Prester John or anyone else ever want to live here?" asked Marko. "It's too hot and too cold and it's impossible to get to. How would their families visit them? How would they get supplies or deliveries or anything?"

Mira nodded. "Do they even have postmen here? Or like, UPS or FedEx?"

"You have to remember that a desert is not just a large dead space," said the tracker. "It breathes and grows and goes through different stages just like any other community. There have been periods when patches of this desert were green and fertile. There have been times when there were not just small towns, but whole cities here. On my map, the area of ruins just ahead of us is called Forty Cities—a whole network of communities once lived here."

Emil joined in. "It's true. My father told me tales of people finding cities in the desert, and not all were abandoned ones—some were quite large, with houses and government buildings and wells and schools."

* * *

After the sun rose high in the sky, threatening to set Mira's hair on fire (or so it felt), Ashok called a halt and got down from his mount. He stopped to look at the map. "We need to make a decision," he said.

Emil slid himself off his camel and walked over to where the tracker was standing in the shade of a lonely coconut palm.

"We can follow this track to a town called Lost, which is about half a day's ride ahead. Or we can leave the path to look in these areas, which are entirely uncharted."

Emil sighed. "I think I can guess which is the most difficult choice, and which is the one we should choose."

Miranda turned to Marko. "We're going off the road."

"If we agree to go to the totally uncharted parts, we still have choices to make. I suggest we head north-northeast," said Ashok. "Another alternative is to go through this mountain pass on the east, but it leads to Nowhere."

Miranda pricked up her ears. "It leads where?"

"Nowhere. Quite literally." He showed her the map. "Look, it's marked in Arabic and Sanskrit, with words that mean 'nowhere' or 'not a place.'"

"That's where we have to go!" cried Mira. "Grandpa said we needed to head to the exact middle of Nowhere. He said we'll find a door in the desert there."

"Hmm. But could he have meant it just as a phrase?" Marko said. "Like you say 'middle of nowhere,' meaning that you're way off the beaten track, like nowheresville?"

Ashok and Emil were both staring at the children. "You speak in such a strange way," the tracker said.

Miranda spoke directly to her brother. "No. I think he meant what he wrote. He wrote Nowhere with a capital *N*, remember? In the middle of Nowhere is where we'll find him." And then she added, for the sake of the others, "And his good friends, Wang Han and Prester John, who will almost definitely be there with him. They're probably waiting with some cold drinks for us."

The two men looked at her, and then at each other. After a pause, the discussion restarted, and the four continued talking for some time. Ashok and Emil were reluctant to follow the children's argument. It sounded too far-fetched. The tracker said, "We can't spend hours or days traveling on a dangerous road to somewhere that is marked on the map as not being a place at all, just because your grandfather made a general comment that might, possibly, be interpreted as referring to it."

But Mira was convinced she was right. "I'm sure it's there. I'm sure that's the place where he wanted us to go. We'll find a door there."

Marko nodded. "He wrote about a place of great wonders, a hidden place, a magical kingdom."

Emil was torn. "Your argument is logical, Ashok. Why travel across a desert to a space shown on the map as empty? But still, I can't help but hear echoes of the rumors of the kingdom of Prester John in the words their grandfather gave them."

Mira was now almost jumping up and down in her desperation to persuade them to head to Nowhere. "All the things we're looking for—Wang Han, Prester John, our grandfather—they all have to be connected somehow. And I'm sure this is where we'll find them."

Ashok scratched his beard, unconvinced. "This place can only have been marked with the word 'Nowhere' because one or more desert people have been there, and found that there was nothing there."

Silence descended. They seemed to be at an impasse.

Then the tracker spoke again. "Let us make a bargain. We travel one day's ride to the center of Nowhere. If we find the people we seek, all well and good. If not, we turn back and follow the road to the town of Lost, get supplies, and then resume our exploration of the northeast for three days."

* * *

And so they remounted their camels and trekked into the space marked on the map as Nowhere.

As the hours drew on, it became obvious why whoever had produced that map had used the words he did. There was quite literally nothing there: no trees, no houses, no birds, no mountains, no valleys. It was a desolate, lifeless plain. Except for some gentle hills, craggy rocks, and an occasional dried-out streambed, it could have been the surface of the moon. There were even craters, just like on the moon.

Mira was sure they were on the right road, and prayed hard that they would see something, anything, that would persuade the two men that this was the right way to go. But every time they went over the top of a gentle, featureless hill, there would be more plains, equally featureless, ahead of them. And all the time it was getting hotter, and there were fewer signs of water.

"What exactly are we looking for?" she asked in a whisper to her brother.

"Don't ask me. Grandpa just said something about a door in the desert."

"But what did he mean by that?"

"I don't know. But it's something right in the middle bit of Nowhere. We need to get to the center of this part of the map."

She called out to Ashok. "Are we in the middle yet?"

He looked up at the sun. "Half an hour's ride to the west will take us to the center," he said.

Just over twenty-five minutes later, they found themselves in a patch of desolate land that looked no different from what had gone before.

The tracker spoke wearily. "OK. This is the middle. And there's nothing here."

Mira looked in all directions. He was right. There was nothing to be seen. Desperately disappointed, she turned to her brother.

Marko was looking to the horizon on his left. "What's that?" he said, pointing.

The others followed his finger but could see nothing but a continuation of the flat plain on which they had traveled.

"There, there. Can you see it?"

Emil rode closer to him and tried to focus on the distance. "What am I supposed to be looking at?"

"Nothing. I mean you can't actually see anything there, but it looks kind of strange."

"Well, if you want me to look at nothing, I can certainly see that."

But Marko remained insistent. "No, look, the nothing is shimmering, ever so slightly. Like the lake before."

Ashok peered forward. "Maybe you're right." He stared for another minute before speaking again. When he spoke again, there was an excitement in his voice, almost a laugh. "I've heard of these, but never seen one before."

"What is it?" Emil asked.

"If it's what I think it is, it's a mirage. But a reverse mirage. Normally, one sees water where there is only dry heat. But my father used to say that there were places in the desert where you saw nothing but dry heat when really there was water. The water is so still, the dust on the surface so thick, the sun so bright, that it looks like nothing—unless by good fortune, something causes movement: a bit of tumbleweed stirs the surface, a breath of wind passes over the top, a bird takes a drink or something."

"There is something there," said Emil, using both hands to shade his eyes. "The sand moves like water. And there are objects on the far side: trees, rocks, something else." He urged his camel forward and started moving toward it. "Let's go see."

Within five minutes, they could see that Ashok had been right—it had been a reverse mirage. In front of them was a perfectly still lake, shimmering in the heat, with a cluster of boulders around it, and some shrubs and short trees lining one side, near some larger rocks.

Even more startling was a gray dot that turned into a seated figure as they approached. He was so still that Miranda was convinced it was a statue.

Then the man rose to his feet as they came within earshot.

"Welcome to the middle of Nowhere," he said. "I've been expecting you."

A Warm Welcome

H ello," said Marko, wanting to be polite. "Er, nice place. How come you speak English?"

"When you came near," said the man, "I saw young, pale faces, and I thought that the best chance to communicate would be in English or Spanish or Chinese or Arabic or Sanskrit, the languages of travelers. I speak them all, a little bit."

"Do you live here?" asked Mira. "But there's no house. You can't live in the open."

"I live where most life is found in the desert—underground."

The four of them dismounted and followed him as he led them to the rocks. Beneath an overhang on one of the larger outcrops was an opening. He led them through it into a dark, damp tunnel where the air was cooler.

"You have air-conditioning?" asked Marko, amazed.

"I don't understand."

"The air's cool inside."

"The air is cool at night, and the tunnel holds on to that coolness for a long time, becoming hot only toward the end of the following day."

Emil and Ashok followed in stunned silence. The man was clearly not Wang Han or Prester John—he was too young for that, barely older than Emil, maybe in his midtwenties.

Ashok spoke to him in Arabic. They spoke for some minutes, and the conversation ended with mutual laughter. The man made a gesture to indicate that they should wait while he fetched something. Then he stepped into a side chamber.

"What are you saying to him?" Emil asked.

"Yeah, it's rude to talk in foreign languages when there's one available that everyone can understand," said Miranda.

The tracker smiled at her haughtiness.

"I asked him why he was so welcoming. After all, a man living alone in the desert would have no defenses if we were a band of thieves. He told me that he often goes for weeks or months without seeing anyone. Occasionally someone will pass, and he usually allows them to pass by without seeing him. But when he saw that our party included children, he decided that we were unlikely to be bandits. He had been praying for some help and saw us as an answer to his prayers. So he tossed a stone into the lake, to capture our attention."

"I'm still finding it hard to believe that we have found someone living this far from civilization," said Emil. "Truly he is a desert dweller."

Ashok nodded his agreement before continuing, "And he's also hoping we can provide him with two things he needs desperately. One is conversation. The other is information."

The young Italian man looked around the chamber, which was furnished with mats made from woven palm-leaf fibers. "I can understand him wanting someone to talk to. But exactly what information is he after? He must know more about this area than anyone else—certainly more than a group of visitors who have just arrived."

The man reappeared with a torch and beckoned them to follow him further into the tunnel. But he extinguished it after five minutes. They could see that there was natural light inside.

"There are several gaps in the rocks above," the desert dweller explained. "They allow natural light to leak into this network of caves. That's why these caves were chosen by the original users, I think. Little light gets down here, but it is bright, so it's fine."

Once they had entered what seemed to be the main room of the dwelling, they sat on palm-frond chairs and shared provisions.

"What do you seek?" the desert dweller asked, directing his comments at the tracker.

"A man. I seek Wang Han," Ashok said. Marko realized that this statement had stunned their host. Not by his reaction—he did not look in the least bit startled—but by his studied lack of reaction. From the moment he heard the name, the dweller moved more slowly, and his expression seemed frozen on his face.

Ashok had apparently also realized this. "I think you seek the same man, am I right, Dorji?"

The man turned slowly and stared at him. "Why do you call me that?" he said.

"Maybe I just made a lucky guess."

"Wait," said Miranda. "Who's Dorji? I mean, who are you?"

Ashok smiled and handed her a piece of flatbread. "Would you like to introduce yourself, Dorji?"

The dweller smiled. "Why don't you do it for me?"

Ashok told the others that Dorji was the first child of Kublai Khan, but had disappeared soon after birth. "They put out the rumor that he was a sickly baby and died as a toddler."

"In reality, they hid me," said the man. "They had heard that there were plots to take over the kingdom. The main two targets would of course have been my father and myself, as the eldest son."

Emil said, "But clearly you did not die as a toddler."

Dorji continued, "I was sent to be raised by a nurse who lived on the corner of this desert. I grew to love it. When my great-uncle Wang Han disappeared, also declared dead, I was suspicious—because of all people, I knew that when a royal leader vanishes, he may merely be hiding from his enemies."

Marko was fascinated. "So you came in search of him?"

"I did. I have spent almost eight years creating a map of the lost towns in this desert."

"We saw the road leading to the Forty Cities," said Ashok.

Dorji smiled. "There have been many more than forty cities here—there have been thousands. Many have come and gone. There are villages on the surface, but also towns below the ground. Almost all are deserted."

The tracker said, "And Wang Han? You haven't found him?"

"Not yet," said Dorji. "He is said to live in a very great underground city, with a large community, and many riches."

He showed them a map of the quadrants of the desert that he had explored. He had searched huge portions of the desert, but there was far more to search. "It will take me more than forty years to search all of it. That's why I seek information. Each traveler whom I welcome will pay for his visit, I hope, by sharing with me information about the parts he has visited."

Ashok got out his own map. "I have the map that shows our route here, but I also have much information about the southern parts of the desert, which have been my playground since I was a boy. You are more than welcome to add this to your store of information."

Dorji nodded. "Good. Come, we will sit together and you will add to my store of knowledge."

"But first," said Emil, "please answer one more question. Do you know anything of the man I seek, a Christian leader named Prester John, who is rumored to live here?"

Dorji smiled. "Of course," he said. "John is another name for Johann. Johann is another name for Wang Han. They are simply different pronunciations of the same name."

Emil looked at Ashok. "So we have been seeking the same man all this time." He turned to the desert dweller. "There are many stories in the West of Prester John, who has a Christian kingdom in the East, and the world's most marvelous collection of treasures."

"One side of our family is indeed Christian, so the tales are more than just stories. As for the treasures … I have yet to find them."

Mira raised her hand to speak, as if she were at school. "Have you seen my grandfather? Has he passed this way? I can show you a photo … I mean … a small painting …"

She opened the locket around her neck and passed it to him.

Their host peered at the tiny image. "The master ... he passed through here three moons ago. He gave me much information, but then he left hurriedly one morning. He was a very knowledgeable man ... but ... also a scared one. It seemed as if he was being pursued. I half expected his pursuers to turn up the following day, but no one came ... until you." Dorji looked at Miranda and at Marko. "You two share his mannerisms."

Miranda grinned and looked at her brother. "We're getting closer," she said.

They drank sweet water from the well. It was good to relax. But they had just settled themselves with blankets on the ground for a nap when a low rumble ran through the room.

Dorji looked up. "That's not good news. Come with me, everybody. Right now."

Temujin's Chamber

"What was that sound?" Miranda asked as she ran.

They followed Dorji as he marched smartly through the tunnels—not the way they had come, but a different route.

"The desert reorganizes itself all the time, every day. Normally, it's just changes on the surface, the dunes moving like the points of waves in the open ocean. But, sometimes, bigger changes happen."

"Like earthquakes?"

"Yes and no. The land moves, but there is no earth here, as such, just rock, sand, and clay. Sometimes a huge area of dunes will 'walk,' traveling together over large distances. Sometimes valleys and mountains swap places. Sometimes, the changes in the surface are big enough and heavy enough to reverberate through to the rocks deep underneath. That's what we can hear."

Miranda and Marko scampered faster.

"We should get out of here," said Emil. "The last place we want to be is in an underground cave."

"The best place to be is close to the surface," said Dorji, "but sheltered, rather than deep underground. And that's fine, because that's where we are going. Do not fear. This one will not be dangerous. It will disappear soon. It will do no harm."

They moved toward a distant light, with the desert dweller slowing down. Before they reached the next chamber, the sound and the shaking had stopped. The desert dweller said, "When I discovered this particular cave four years ago, I realized that it was a sort of gatehouse to the hidden cities in the desert."

"What does that mean?" Mira asked.

"People searching for the lost city will find nothing. It is too well hidden. A tiny number may find this place. They are given supplies and information by the keepers and then sent home. The original keepers have died, and so, I am now the keeper of the gatehouse. Once travelers realize that it will take forty years of searching to have any hope of finding the hidden entrance to the city, they are happy to give up and go home."

"Forty years!" said Emil. "And I thought my family were serious explorers."

They slipped through a narrow opening into another chamber. This one led to a strange sight—rows of shoes neatly arranged in lines next to one cave wall.

"Those are cute," said Mira. She reached for one pair. They crumbled into dust in her hands, as if they were made of sand.

"They are old," Dorji said. "Very old."

"Whose were they?"

"That's a question I asked myself for days after I first found this place. Who took their shoes off here—and why did no one return for them?"

He moved to a different part of the room and then disappeared into the shadows. "And then I found this secret door."

They followed him into pitch-black shadows. They heard movement and saw sparks as Dorji lit a torch. The light let them see that they were in a storehouse of some sort, containing scrolls and carvings.

"This is an archive of the history of Asia. It includes much material about my great-grandfather, Genghis Khan. In this chamber we find stored many of his artifacts from the early years."

Marko picked up another pair of shoes—they were small, about the size of his own feet. "Whose are these?" he asked. The shoes did not crumble, so they seemed less old than the ones outside.

"Genghis Khan started his career very young," the desert dweller explained. "He was a boy named Temujin, about nine years old when his father died. By the time he was sixteen, he was the leader of a tribe."

"Was he from the desert?" asked Miranda.

"No, from the north of China, the land of the Mongols. By the time he was twenty-eight, he had united the tribes and become the leader of many. He went on to conquer most of the lands of this world."

Emil nodded, "But they say he was a bloodthirsty man."

"True. He killed the adult males and took the women and children as slaves."

"When did his name change?" Marko asked.

"It never did. People still remember him as Temujin, and Genghis Khan is a title—it means Lord of the Universe."

The three men stayed up late, adding details to Dorji's map, with each point being discussed endlessly, sometimes in several languages.

Mira found her eyes getting heavy, so she crawled into a corner with her blanket and decided to sleep. She looked at the magic mirror, to see if the guardian was inside. She saw nothing but her own tired eyes.

* * *

What seemed like mere minutes later, light was coming into the room. The night had passed. It was morning.

Mira rose and found that everyone else was up and preparing to ride on the next leg of the journey.

While there were still more than a thousand quadrants of the desert that needed to be explored, Dorji had identified a small number that he proposed they explore as a group.

His face had grown serious as he spoke. "In particular, there are a few places that have rumors attached to them—rumors of trouble, of death and destruction."

Mira's eyebrows rose as she saw his logic. "Oh, great, the safe ones you do by yourself, the dangerous ones you do with us, so that if someone gets killed, it's not necessarily you."

Ashok held up his hand to silence her. "Girl, what you say may be true, but still, this is good strategy. If you are working alone, the amount of risk you can take is limited. If there is a group, you can take more risks."

"Why don't you save those really difficult places for times when a heavily armed army is with you?" she asked. "Instead of two men and two children?"

Dorji surprised her by smiling. "Young lady, that's a good point. I should go with the biggest army I can put together, but two men and two children are the biggest army I have ever managed to assemble in this place." He smiled.

Marko, ever the practical one, wanted details. "Can you tell us about the rumors? What difficulties will we face? Where are we going? Are we going to have to fight bad guys?"

Dorji turned to face him. "Let me share with you some news that came to me just three days ago. Late one night, I heard the strains of heavy breathing coming from a long distance away. Sound travels far in these parts, in certain weather conditions. I went out searching and found a traveler, driven half-mad by heat and exhaustion."

He stroked his beard thoughtfully. "The man said that he had been with a party of four people crossing the Taklamakan. They reached a place where there was another world, one that they could see plainly in the sky."

"Another world? You mean like the moon?"

"Yes, but very close. He said they could see the buildings and even people walking around in that world. But all this was in the sky. The city was upside-down—a mirror of an Earth city. Yet no one fell off it."

Emil stared at Ashok.

Miranda spoke: "So he claimed he saw a city, upside down, in the sky, with people walking around in it, but not falling off?"

"Correct."

"Weird."

"Clearly his time in the desert had driven him not half-mad, but completely insane," said Ashok. "This is impossible, for sure. Did you believe his story?"

Dorji thought for a moment before continuing. "I distrusted him in one sense. What he said was clearly impossible, all of us would agree. He could not have seen what he claimed to have seen, but at the same time, he was telling the truth. He believed what came from his mouth."

"Did you check it out," asked Miranda. "I mean, did you go have a look?"

Dorji's face grew serious again. "He told me it was a place of great danger. There had been four men in his party. All had lost their lives except for him."

"So that's why you were so welcoming. You wanted buddies to go to this dangerous place with you," Miranda said.

Emil had a question. "My father and uncle are great travelers and have spoken of many great wonders, but a city, upside down in the sky? This is something they have never spoken of. It cannot be possible."

Silence followed these words. And then came an unexpected comment from the youngest member of the group.

"Not necessarily."

Everyone turned to look at Marko. The small boy smiled. "It could be an inversion caused by light refraction. There's a page on this in my *Big Book of Weather*."

There was a long pause. Then Emil said, "Explain, please."

"Well, I'm not sure if I remember all the details."

"Just try," said Mira, impatiently. "In words of one syllable, please."

The boy screwed up his face, as he did when he was thinking hard.

"Well, it's like this. When the air is dry, and suddenly there is a lot of moisture in a particular part of the atmosphere, the light bends. The result is that you can see things where they aren't. For example, there may be a city in one place, but you'll see it in another place."

Mira looked blank. "I don't get it."

"It's the same principle that creates rainbows. Light moving from one place to another is bent and made visible in the air … that kind of thing."

The men said nothing.

As earnest as ever, Marko continued: "Over the years, there have been lots of cases of people seeing cities or mountains or stuff floating in the air. There was a case recently in China, where people could see a city in the sky for several hours. There are pictures of it on the internet. Er, the Internet is a place where pictures and things are gathered where we come from. Anyway, sometimes the image is upside down, depending on how the light is bent. The air acts like a prism. Do you know what a prism is?"

Nobody spoke. Then Ashok turned to Dorji. "This child is special," he said. "He sounds crazy, but he knows much. It is hard to understand his words, but he has a gift. He may indeed be a *natha deyyo*, or some such creature."

Dorji nodded, "I have heard of such children."

Marko objected, "Look, it's nothing. I just read a lot."

Mira said, "Yeah, he reads A LOT."

14

City in the Sky

The place where two worlds met was a full day's travel away. There would be a half day's ride, a midday stop at an oasis known by Dorji, a further ride of several hours, until at last, a final stand before the gateway to a hidden world, what he called the Watchtower of the Secret Sands. It was a building that marked the entrance to a pathway of long tunnels that led under the desert to the vantage point where they could see the city in the sky.

The first part of the journey was uneventful. Dorji shared stories about his family. Marko wished he had a pen to write them all down. The family was a curious mix of nationalities, cultures, and personalities.

Genghis Khan, the patriarch, saw nothing wrong with slaughtering huge numbers of people, but there were other members of his family who were calm, religious people who spent their time providing services for the needy. These were Christians and Buddhists. Genghis Khan also spread his kingdom southward, and his family members there had good relations with Hindu and Muslim groups too.

After several hours in the sun, the conversation died down, and all five of them dozed on the backs of the camels as the beasts plodded through the sand. Everyone was delighted when they reached the gateway: the Watchtower of the Secret Sands.

It was a sand-colored pagoda, three stories high, placed on a raised, flat area of rock. Stairs led up to the opening.

The camels were given rest and shelter, and the group went into an underground warren to rest and have a drink.

"Thank goodness you know about these places," Ashok said.

"I know about them only because of the gathered knowledge of thousands of explorers like yourselves," said Dorji.

* * *

The afternoon light was waning when they got to the stop where they could leave their camels. The last part of the journey was a long walk through a tunnel.

"It'll be cooler and less dangerous this way," Dorji explained.

The tunnels were certainly cooler, partly because they were sheltered from the sun, except for occasional light vents, and partly because they often got linked with underground rivers that sent moisture through them.

Still, it was a tiring journey, and Marko was glad when a shout from the front indicated that they had reached their destination.

"If we emerge here, we should be close enough to see it," Dorji said.

The five of them clambered out of a gap between some huge boulders. Although darkness was falling, there was still enough light to see the sky above them, which was completely clear.

Ashok spoke first. "So where is it? This city in the sky."

"Right there," said Dorji. He pointed to a direction close to where the sun was about to set.

Marko, who was feeling disappointed, asked the

obvious question. "So why can't we see it?"

Dorji shrugged. "The man told me that it becomes visible when the sun is three fingers above the horizon." He stretched out his hand toward the sun. "Which it will be very soon."

Mira stretched out her own hand toward the sun. "Three fingers? How do you work that out?"

"I guess their arms are longer than ours, and their fingers fatter," said Marko. "It must be measured by the hands of a grown-up."

As they stood waiting, a sense of awe came over them. The sky in the desert was so vast. The horizon was so distant, and yet so unchanging. From the center of this huge plain, it really seemed as if the world was a massive, flat, circular plane, a disk floating in space.

Marko could immediately see why most of the world's great religions started in deserts and mountains. Here you felt tiny and yet you felt connected to something huge, to the universe, to God, to everything.

A gasp came from his left. Miranda put her hand to her mouth. "It's coming. I can see it," she said. "I can see it."

As the five of them watched, a city came into focus in the sky. And as promised, everything was upside down.

The buildings, the trees, the hills, were all somehow affixed in place to a hard brown surface in the air.

Marko noticed some moving dots. "I can see people," he said. "They're walking upside down. This is cool. They look like they should fall off."

"Small boy," said Dorji. "You said you had some explanation for this."

"Er, yes, it's hard to explain, though. The moisture in the air bends the light. It's called an inversion."

Ashok stepped over to Marko. "It is hard to understand your words. But answer this simple question. Is it a vision? Or is it a real city? Can we get there?"

The boy nodded. "Oh yes. The city isn't really in the sky. It's on the ground. It's reflected onto water vapor in the air."

Emil was excited. "We can get there? How do we do that?"

"Just head straight for it, at ground level," said Marko. "Since the sun is setting over there, that's the direction you'd need to go."

Dorji said, "This place is dangerous, I'm sure. We will rise soon after midnight. We'll head to the city in the early hours of the morning. We need to get there before dawn."

Miranda was in a deep sleep when Ashok woke her, but she found herself immediately wide awake. "OK. I'll be up in a sec," she said. "And I'll get Marko up."

Her heart was pounding. She looked around in the dark. Her brother was still fast asleep.

Creeping across the room, she took the magic mirror out of the backpack and went to hide with it in a corner.

"Are you there, guardian?" she whispered. Why had the mysterious voice abandoned her after that one visit on her first night in this land? Had she dreamed it all?

She focused her eyes hard and found that she could once more look into it—the mirror seemed to open up and become a three-dimensional space. As she stared, her reflection vanished and she could see a hazy image of a network of rooms inside: the place where the guardian was. But details were hard to see. It was like looking through the windows of a vehicle that had crossed the dustiest plains of Africa without stopping at a single car wash.

There was nobody there.

She decided to try and re-create the journey on which the guardian had taken her. Standing up with the mirror in front of her, she took four or five steps forward to look at the items that had been lined along the back wall in the land the guardian called "the other side."

She found the alcove containing her grandfather's hourglass. It had changed. It was much brighter. And the top half was no longer almost empty. It was filled with glowing grains of sand.

"Thank goodness," she said out loud. "We must have done something right." She realized that simply by getting the map this close to him, they must have somehow already greatly improved his chances of living longer. He had many more choices in his life, represented by the many more grains of sand.

She was about to put the mirror down when she felt curious about something. What about her own hourglass? Surely the glass of her life must be around here somewhere? Why not take a look at it? Given her age, the top half must be packed with sand—she was only just beginning her life, after all.

She angled the mirror around. She could see other alcoves, but they swam in and out of focus. She felt guilty, knowing she probably wasn't meant to be doing this. Would the guardian be angry with her?

She paused, but only for a few seconds. She found the temptation impossible to resist. That's when she saw an alcove to the left of her grandfather's one and moved toward it. "Show me our life-glasses, show me our life-glasses," she chanted in a whisper.

Inside the alcove she saw two more hourglasses. They were almost empty! She looked at the names on top of them: Miranda Lee and Marko Lee.

She gasped.

They were almost empty.

She stared first at her own hourglass, getting as close to it as she could. The top half of each glass had just a few grains left—and they were disappearing fast, vanishing into the nothingness of the bottom half. She turned to Marko's glass. It was the same.

There could only be one meaning. Danger! They were close to death.

Suddenly something green slammed in front of what she could see. She heard a hissing sound. The mirror burned in her hands, as if an electric shock had traveled through it. She dropped it.

It lay on the ground, suddenly nothing more than a flat piece of decorated metal.

She turned to Marko and woke him up. "Wake up, wake up. We're in danger. We've got to get out of here."

He rose up groggily. "What's the problem?"

"I can't explain, but I saw something in the mirror. Our lives are about to come to an end. We have to leave, right now."

"What about delivering the map to Grandpa?"

Mira stopped. They had to complete their mission. What could they do? "We'll give the map to Emil to take to Grandpa. We have to turn back."

They raced up to the main chamber, where they found the three men. Dorji had lit the room with torches.

Mira went to one corner where Emil was swinging his arms to get his blood circulation moving. "I need to talk to you," Miranda said. "We're not going to the city."

"But you are so close. And you want so much to find your grandfather."

She nodded. "We'd like to see him, but we can't. He wrote us a letter. It says that we should bring something to him. But it says that we should not go ourselves. He said it would be too dangerous for us. I ignored it—but now I realize that he must have been right."

"What is it? Do you want me to take it to him?"

"Yes. Will you?" She showed him the map they had found in the second drawer of Grandpa's second desk.

She looked around to see that Ashok had been listening to the conversation. "You're not coming? That's probably wise. But where will you go?" the tracker asked. "I think you must wait here for our return."

"I don't know," the girl said. "Maybe. Or maybe we can find some other people who will take us with—"

Suddenly the ground shook violently below them.

All of them except Dorji fell to the floor. "This is a bad one," said the desert dweller. "We must move. That way—out of the tunnel, everybody run, NOW."

Mira watched as the adults started to move in one direction. But where was her brother? She looked around. She saw that Marko had moved the opposite way, racing deeper into the cave.

"Tell your brother to come back," Ashok shouted. "He's going the wrong way."

"Marko!" Mira screamed. "Come back!"

But the boy continued to run into the network of tunnels.

Mira pushed the envelope containing grandfather's map into Emil's hands. "Take this to my grandfather. You can open it. It'll help you on your journey. Please, you must deliver it to the man whose name is on the front."

"You need to escape—this is the only way out," Emil said.

Mira took a deep breath. Should she escape from the collapsing tunnels by running outside with the others? Or follow Marko? But if she went after her brother, wouldn't that mean certain death? Was this what the empty life-glasses meant? That she and her brother were about to lose their lives in this tunnel?

"Come," said Emil.

"I must go with my brother," she replied, making the decision at the same time as the words came from her mouth.

She turned and ran after Marko. Behind her, she heard Ashok shouting. "Come back. You cannot survive."

"There are no other ways out," shouted Dorji.

Mira ran into the darkness. Behind her, in front of her, under her, and over her, she heard grinding noises as the underground network of tunnels began to collapse in on itself.

She realized she was about to die.

15

The End of the Tunnel

Miranda ran after her crazy brother, a white blur far ahead of her.

"Where are you going? The tunnel's collapsing from all sides," she shrieked. "We can't escape this way. We have to turn back."

He looked back but kept running.

She ran as fast as she could. Now the rumbling was right behind her, rocks rolling down near her heels. She could hear great screeching noises as massive boulders came loose behind her, sending clouds of dust through the tunnels.

The light from behind disappeared completely. Now she knew that the only way out was sealed shut.

Having no options left, she just kept running. If we're going to die, she thought, we might as well die together. It was hard to see her brother in the reduced light seeping through the few remaining cracks in the ceiling of the tunnel.

But then she raced around one corner and saw him turn to the right. She followed. Turning one more corner, to the left this time, she could see that he had come to a halt. He was standing in a shaft of light looking upward.

"Marko, we're trapped," she said. "We can't get out." The rumbling grew louder. The floor below them started shaking.

"Yes we can," he said. "That's our way out. I noticed it earlier when we passed by."

Then she saw it.

Up through a light vent in the top of the tunnel a small patch of night sky was visible. And it contained a full moon.

Suddenly she realized what his plan was.

Fumbling in the backpack, she pulled out the magic mirror. Together they held it up so that the moonlight shone through it.

At first, nothing happened. And then Miranda saw Grandpa's life-glass through the filter—the amount of sand had grown again. Her decision to give the map to Emil to deliver had been the right move.

They felt the mirror crackle with electricity, and the quality of light coming through the thin metal filter changed. It became increasingly bright. And then there was a flash.

* * *

Marko automatically closed his eyes. His tightly shut eyelids were filled with a bright white glare, which slowly faded to a dull gray. That's when he opened them, one at a time.

They were at home, in their grandfather's study.

"Phew," breathed Mira.

"Phew indeed," said Marko.

"That was close."

"Yes."

Slowly, the boy walked over to their grandfather's chair and sat down. He breathed out a long sigh. "I think I need to rest."

Mira could hardly speak. "You said it," she said in a small voice. Paralyzed with fear, she could barely move.

But then they heard a noise—someone was moving around outside.

"We've got visitors, remember?" Marko said. "Why don't you open the door?"

There was a knock at the study door. It was Mr. Aldred, Mira knew.

"May I come in?" said the teacher's voice.

The girl, clearly having no strength to resist, slowly turned toward the door, but she didn't have the energy to open it.

The handle turned and it swung open. The tall, scary math teacher stepped into the room.

She gave him a wide, fake smile. "Why, Mr. Aldred, what a surprise to see you here," she said, working hard to sound natural. "Er, I'm afraid Mama and Daddy have just popped out for a minute. I mean for a few minutes, not that long, but probably too long for you to wait. But I'll tell them you popped in. After you've gone. Thanks for coming. Bye."

"How did you get the key?" Marko asked.

"Anya gave it to me. She told me to pop in and give you this," he said, holding out a bag. "I did knock a couple of times. I guess you didn't hear me."

Marko wondered who Anya was, but said nothing.

Mira took the bag from him. "Thank you."

"She said you ate a lot of ice cream, and you might like something to go with it."

At that, Marko hopped off the chair to go and look at the gift. Inside the bag was a large cake box—and through the transparent window in the lid, a huge chocolate cake was visible.

"Wow. Thanks. Who's Anya?" he asked.

Mr. Aldred laughed. "Oh, sorry. You know her as Ms. Modi, the art teacher. I call her Anya, or 'the wife.'"

Mira's eyes widened. "You're married to Ms. Modi?"

"Didn't you know? I guess not. You gave her the keys to your house, right? She would have come herself, but she's got her book club meeting tonight, so she passed it to me."

Mira was speechless.

The teacher smiled. "You didn't know we were married? Don't look so surprised. Is it that hard to imagine?" He laughed. "Perhaps it is. I guess we're pretty different. She's tiny, I'm tall. She's easygoing, I'm on the strict side."

"You can say that again."

He chuckled again. "Well, Anya sees something worth cultivating in me, and she's a woman of great taste in friendships. You and I must agree on that, at least? So maybe I'm not all bad. Anyway, having made my delivery, I'll be off."

* * *

Marko was looking worried. "Did we fail in our mission this time?"

"No," said Miranda. "We were meant to deliver the map to Grandpa, and we did. Emil got it to him. I know he did."

"How do you know?"

"I just have a feeling," she said, not wanting to reveal that she had been peering into the world of the mirror. There was something inside that seemed dangerous. The green eyes that she had seen several times—who did they belong to? Was it a friend or foe? He referred to himself as the guardian, but who or what was he guarding? Was he an angel or a devil?

"I really wanted to meet Prester John," said Marko. "See if all the legends were true."

Miranda sat down and peered at the magic mirror. She spoke without looking at her brother. "I bet one day we will," she said. "And I bet we'll meet Emil and Ashok again. I think it's our destiny. This story isn't over."

She looked at the edge of the magic mirror. A new Chinese character had appeared on the edge of it.

"A new character?" Marko asked.

"Yes," said Miranda.

"Let's investigate it later."

She nodded. "It think it's time for an ice cream and chocolate cake break. What do you think?"

"Sounds good to me."

They walked to the kitchen, their footsteps quickening at the thought of dessert.

A Note from the Authors

Many of the historical and scientific facts in this book are true. By reading it, you've learned about life in Asia in the 1200s. Here are some of the things that really happened.

The Taklamakan Desert is real, and can be found in Central Asia, in the Xinjiang Province of China. There really is an "orchestra of dust" that produces drumming sounds and noises like singing in the desert.

Although the meetings and dates in this story are fictional, Marco Polo, Dorji Khan, and Wang Han were all real people who lived in the 1200s.

The description of dry rivers of sand floating in the desert come from old writings about the place. So does the tale of the slippers that crumble to dust when they are touched. As do the legends of the lost cities, and the method of extracting water from the sand.

Part of the family of famous conqueror Genghis Khan was Christian, and this may have given rise to the legend of Prester John, leader of a mysterious Christian kingdom in the Orient.

Marco Polo's family was known as the Emiliones, and the book that was eventually written about his travels was first called *Il Milione*, although it later became generally known as *The Travels of Marco Polo*.

Mirages of cities in the sky are real, and have been seen in many countries.

Although Miranda and Marko Lee are fictional characters, the Magic Mirror books are a fun way to learn the most exciting real-life stories of the past. And most amazing of all, the magic mirror itself is a real artifact from China. See if you can find a picture of one on the Internet.

—*Luther Tsai and Nury Vittachi*

About the Authors

Luther Tsai has achievements worldwide as an architect, urban planner, author, and academic. From creating spaces in the most vibrant cities of modern Asia to creating innovative humanities, science, English, and Mandarin curriculums worldwide, Luther and his wife, Serene Pang, the education consultant for this series, re-create the remarkable vision of ancient Asia found in the Magic Mirror series.

Nury Vittachi is an author based in Hong Kong. His writing is "endearingly wacky," said *The Times of London*, and "heading for cult status," according to the *Herald Sun* of Melbourne, Australia. Vittachi has had regular broadcasting slots on the BBC and CNN. *Doctor Who* star David Tennant recently recorded an audiobook version of a Vittachi tale.